CW01457044

Death of a Viewer

Herbert Adams

Death of a Viewer

Copyright © 2022 Indo-European Publishing

All rights reserved

The present edition is a reproduction of previous publication of this classic work. Minor typographical errors may have been corrected without note; however, for an authentic reading experience the spelling, punctuation, and capitalization have been retained from the original text.

ISBN: 978-1-64439-969-9

1

Conspiracy

"Sandra, we are broke."

"More than usual?"

"Infinitely more. Finally, definitely and completely broke."

"What is it—cards or racing?"

"Both, and something on the Stock Exchange. I am sorry, darling, but never in my life have I known such damnable ill-luck. Everything at once. To get square I plunged on Last Chance for the big race. It was a cert and it won. But the jockey was disqualified. That put the lid on."

There was no reply. The room was luxurious rather than poverty-stricken and the two people in it showed no signs of penury. It was an apartment in a South Kensington hotel. Not perhaps the most fashionable quarter in that area—if there is one—but its charges were high and its appointments adequate.

The man perched on the arm of a well-padded settee looked less rueful than his words might have suggested. He had good features and dark wavy hair. He was in evening clothes of the latest style, complete except that he had not yet donned his "tails." His trousers, shirt and shoes left nothing to be desired. The girl, sitting in front of the mirror, was using her lipstick. Over her dainty underwear she had a quilted, silken bed jacket, partially fastened. The dress she was to wear lay on the bed. From his perch the man could see her reflection in the glass, the curves of her neck and the fine contours of her breasts. He could also see himself. They were in fact as good-looking a couple as one could easily find. He noted with pleasure, as he always did, her feminine shapeliness, her golden hair and clear blue eyes. He was watching the expression on her face. It had not changed as he told of his misfortunes and when she spoke her voice showed no emotion.

"How exactly do we stand?" she said at last.

"As the bankruptcy people, unfeeling brutes, will put it—liabilities

£4,000, assets nil. I have enough cash to keep us here for another two or three weeks but I owe a tidy bit to Marcus Galloway. Nothing further doing there. Have you anything?"

"The price of a cab fare. My little bit gone?"

She could see his head as he nodded. "I am afraid, darling, everything is gone."

There was another uneasy silence. How would she take it? He watched her anxiously, as well he might.

"I was a fool to marry you, Ossie." The words were still cool. "I suppose all girls have that sort of madness when they are young. With some it turns out all right. They get the prizes. I got only—you."

"You enjoyed it while it lasted."

"Five years," she murmured.

He got up and kissed her shoulder. "Darling, I still love you and we have each other."

She made no response. Broke! The word was familiar enough to her. Her parents had been strolling players, as it was once called, or members of touring companies in more modern parlance. They were not good enough to get London engagements of any value, and although not often out of work there had been times when only loans from their friends kept them going. They had hoped for great things from her, but she had disappointed them. They got her chances but her talents did not lie that way.

"You have the looks, Sandra," her mother sometimes told her, "far better than most girls, but you say the words as though you were reading a story. You must be it, you must live it."

"She may wake up when she falls in love," her father had said. They both died when she was seventeen. She got a job as a model in a W End dressmaking establishment and her poise and her promising figure gave her some success. Before she was nineteen she met and married Captain Oswald Henshaw.

She thought she loved him and she imagined he was rich, He certainly spent money freely. She heard mention of five thousand pounds and supposed that was his annual income. She did not know it was his entire capital, left him by his father, and he was busy getting rid of it as quickly as he could. It is a tribute perhaps to his skill as a gambler—or to his luck—that it had lasted so long. At his suggestion she had put her modest savings, about three hundred pounds, into what he called their joint account so that they could both draw on it. Now that was gone, too. Luckily she had no debts, her parents had at least taught her the folly of that.

"I suppose I can go back to old Harbottle," she said at last. "What will you do?"

"I don't want you to go back to Harbottle, darling, to wear his rags from evening gowns to swim suits and be stared at by the other women and the men they bring with them, like a prize beast at a show."

"That is how we met."

"I took you from it. I don't want you to go back."

"What will you do?" she asked again, perhaps with a show of derision.

"What can I do? I would like the sort of job Tony Somers got—secretary to a rich American who really only wanted to see the high spots. But such chances are few and far between."

"You have your car."

"It went on Last Chance. I must hand it over at the end of the month. I sold my pearl studs too; these are fake."

"You never told me."

"It has been pretty sudden, my dear. I hoped to the last to get square."

Again there was silence. Her hands dropped to the dressing-table. They looked at each other in the mirror, perhaps as they had never done before. She had loved him and she was not very worldly-wise. She had realised for some months that things were not going well with them, but she had never thought they would be as bad as this. Perhaps it was the loss of her small savings that hurt most. She had accumulated them so slowly, so carefully, with a good deal of self-denial, in the days before she married "wealth." Something for a rainy day had been one of her father's maxims, even if he could seldom live up to it. Now, without a word to her, all was gone, gone with nothing to show for it to a bookmaker already over-rich.

"One hears on all hands that men are wanted," she said slowly.

"Men of experience, darling. What can I do? You would not have me drive a bus or tend a bar?"

3

She did not answer. After a time he spoke again.

"As a matter of fact I have a plan, but it needs your help."

"What is it?"

"You know Ewen Jones?"

"Of course I do."

"He admires you tremendously."

She turned from the mirror and faced him.

"You have sold everything you possess, Ossie. If you think of selling me you must find someone with a lot more money than Ewen Jones." There was contempt in her tone.

"It is not that at all, darling. You may be the only precious thing left to me but I would not lose you for all the gold in the world. It hurts me that you should for a moment suggest such a thing."

"Then what are we talking about?"

"You say Ewen is not rich. That of course is true. He is a Member of Parliament—"

"For some squalid place in the East End."

"Yes, but it means nearly two thousand a year. I was at school with him and we were in the army together. His father, formerly Jimmie Jones and now Lord Bethesda, was as fiery Socialist as you could find in all Wales. Then they put him in the House of Lords and he married Connie Marden, the only daughter of the late Josiah Marden, the brewer. Josiah's father or grandfather started with a single pub but they acquired more and started brewing. When he died Josiah left something over half a million to his daughter after all duties had been paid."

"And if what Ewen says is true," Sandra commented, "Lady Bethesda still keeps a tight hand on it. How does this interest us?"

"When Socialists get into the House of Lords," her husband smiled, "they often tend to moderate their opinions. When they marry wealthy women the process may be quicker. Connie would not accept him if he kept the old name as many of them do. Lord Jones would sound a little foolish. So they became Lord and Lady Bethesda, after the place where he was born."

"How does this interest us?" Sandra repeated. "Ewen has little to do

4

with his stepmother and his opinions are as strong as his father's used to be. His wife thinks like he does."

"His wife?"

"Gwennie Wren. I know she writes and speaks in her own name but she is his wife."

"How do you know that?" Ossie asked, smiling again.

"Isn't it true?"

"I very much doubt it, though it might be better if it were so. Certainly they have lived together for a time in that queer place in dockland, but marriage may or may not have come into it. They do not always agree and he is very tired of her. I don't blame him. You cannot have two tub-thumpers in one house, each trying to shout down the other."

"Is this leading anywhere?" Sandra asked.

"Yes, darling. One thing I want to make clear. Connie Bethesda has piles of pelf and oceans of pride. She would pay handsomely to prevent any breath of scandal coming to her family, or rather to the family she had honoured with her alliance."

"There is scandal already if Ewen and Gwennie Wren live together and are not married."

"East is east and west is west. Dockland to Connie is much farther away than the Riviera or New York. She only knows of Gwen as a writer of society gossip with a tendency to poisonous socialism. She keeps away from such things; won't allow them to be mentioned."

"What about Ewen's father?"

"If he knows or suspects anything he is too wise to tell his wife about it. The thing is this. Ewen admires you. If you encouraged him a little he would fall for you completely. If I discovered you and him in what we will call compromising circumstances and threatened an action for the alienation of my wife's affection Connie would pay up handsomely to settle out of court. You and I, happily reconciled, would be in clover."

Sandra looked at him for some moments without speaking. It would have been difficult for anyone to tell what she was thinking. In the curious world in which she had been brought up strict morality had been more conspicuous by its absence than its rigid observance.

"Say that again," she said slowly.

"I am not suggesting there should be anything wrong," Ossie replied. "I could not allow that. Heaven forbid. But if Ewen made love to you, as he would like to do, I see no reason why he or his family should not pay for it. It is just a little drama in which you and I would play our parts and it should have a happy ending. I believe in happy endings!"

"A sort of blackmail?"

"Not in the least, darling. I should demand nothing. I said I should threaten an action. If they offered me something not to bring it I should be forced to listen to them. Not only the slur on the noble Bethesda name would be involved but Ewen would be dropped by the party and lose his seat. With two thousand we could carry on. Connie might be good for ten."

"I never thought you were such a blackguard, Ossie."

"I am not. Desperate ills call for desperate remedies, that is all. Can you suggest anything better? You do not want me to drive a bus?"

She did not answer the question. She said, "If Ewen and Gwennie Wren are married Gwen might bring the action against Ewen and me. That would not help you. Lady Bethesda would not pay for mud already thrown."

"Clever of you, Sandra, to have thought of that. I had not overlooked it, but Ewen and Gwen are not married and never will be. I assure you that is a fact. She wants to have a life of her own. So does he. He is ambitious, and as I told you he is tired of her. You cannot have two kings in one castle."

"You are his friend."

"Of course I am! That is what makes it so bad for him to covet my wife."

Again she looked at him as though seeking to read the thoughts behind his smile. She did not doubt the truth of what he said about Ewen and Gwen. His plan would be so foolish if it were otherwise. She spoke slowly.

"I think I understand. Would you put your proposals in writing, promising me half of anything you receive?"

He stared at her. Then he laughed.

"I never thought you were mercenary, Sandra."

"I am not," she said. "But I am learning."

6

"Of course I could not write anything like that. If you lost it, if anyone else got hold of it, we should be cooked. Might be charged with conspiracy."

"That is what I thought." She again spoke very slowly. "Suppose I really fell for Ewen?"

He bent forward and kissed her.

"I am not afraid of that. He is too stodgy for you and you love me. Come along, darling. We are late already. Slip on your frock and we will go to Pegano's for a drink. To the end of our troubles! We might meet him there and you could start the good work!"

2

Old Nick's Folly

Roger Bennion became involved in what was to be known as the Television Murder in rather a curious manner. His father, old Sir Christopher, before and after the First World War had added to his considerable wealth by judicious speculations in house property. The ground leases of houses in fashionable Belgravia were getting very short. Built nearly a hundred years before, many of them were still in their primeval state. Noble families had houses without bathrooms, or at most with one. They lacked electric light and the servants' quarters were dark and dismal.

Sir Christopher was able to buy them for a few pounds—in some cases they paid substantial sums to be relieved of the liability to redecorate and put them in repair. On undertaking to bring them up to modern standards he secured new and longer leases. Then three or four bathrooms, central heating, up-to-date sanitation, dinner lifts, parquet floors, tasteful decorations and, where necessary, bigger windows were installed. He had a genius for such things and only asked a reasonable profit on his outlay. He found a ready market.

He felt he was doing a good work, but when the housing problem became acute and domestic help almost disappeared he turned his attention to country properties. Many an old manor house became adapted as a school, a convalescent home, or was cut up into flats. He also created what some called Old Nick's Folly.

It was nothing of the sort. It was a deliberate attempt to offer houses to disabled soldiers, sailors or civilians at rents they could afford, regardless of the losses he thereby incurred. He saw it as a thank-offering for a long and successful life. Many people in the past had left money to endow almshouses. He thought it better in his lifetime to erect them and have the pleasure of seeing the right folk enjoy them, not as almshouses but as homes of which they could be proud. An example others might emulate.

He bought some land not far from the London docks and built between thirty and forty little dwellings of tasteful design with labour-saving comforts and conveniences. Each had a small garden and was let to a suitable tenant at a rent of six shillings a week, with the landlord paying the rates and doing the repairs. He lost heavily on them but it was his little village and became a cheery oasis amid the grime and squalor of its surroundings. He might have done more in the same way but building restrictions, higher costs and his own increasing age prevented it.

As his second name was Nicholas many laughed at him and the enterprise became known as Old Nick's Folly.

He had a reliable agent to look after the property but he liked his son Roger, who had been his partner in some of his ventures, though not in that, to visit there occasionally and report personally to him. It thus happened that on the day after Ossie Henshaw announced his financial difficulties to Sandra his wife, Roger was strolling amid the freshly painted cottages, mostly bright with gay flowers.

At one of them he stopped. As he did so the occupant, a big and certainly able-bodied man, came out.

"Major Bennion," he boomed. "Pleasure to see you here. An unusual pleasure if I may say so."

"I came to see you," Roger said.

"I am honoured. Come inside."

Roger followed him into a pleasant room that served as sitting-room and study. Meals were generally eaten in the neat, little kitchen behind it. Upstairs were two bedrooms and a bathroom.

"Sit down, Major Bennion. What can I do for you?"

"Do you know a man named Daniel Floss?"

"Old Dan, my father's gardener?"

"I believe so."

"Of course I know him," was the hearty reply. "An excellent fellow, though I fear his gardening days are done. Crippled with arthritis. Getting on in years, too."

"So I understand. His wife is a decent woman?"

"Excellent, excellent. I believe she still helps sometimes in the house."

"They have been recommended," Roger said, "as a suitable couple for one of these cottages. They have friends here. Your father wants their present cottage for a new and younger man, and is willing to help them get something else."

"Quite right. You could not have worthier people. Worked hard and I would like them to end their days in a nice little place like one of these."

He spoke heartily. He had a big voice and possessed a thick crop of curly, reddish-brown hair over a strongly featured face. His age was about thirty-five. "I can recommend them in every way," he added.

"I am glad of that, Mr. Jones," Roger said. "The trouble is we have nothing available for them. I was wondering if you would move out and let them come here?"

"That is not quite reasonable, is it?"

"Very reasonable, I think. You, as a Member of Parliament, are not the sort of person these places were meant for."

"Maybe, maybe not. Here I am and here I stay." Ewen grinned as one who knew his rights. "If it is a question of rents you will find me open to a fair settlement."

"As you should know," Roger replied, "it is nothing of that sort. My father intended these to be homes for the veterans of the services, or of industry generally. You got this by a sort of trick. You knew the Maxwells, a worthy old couple. When Maxwell had to go to hospital you suggested to his wife that you should come as a lodger. What you paid would help her. Lodgers, by the way, are not allowed or each house might take them, perhaps several of them, and the nature of the place would be changed. When Maxwell died you stayed on with Mrs. Maxwell as your housekeeper. When she died some months later you still stayed on. Mason, my father's agent, unfortunately accepted rent from you—"

"And so created a tenancy," the M.P. smiled. "I know the law on these things. If you wanted to live here yourself—"

"I do not. I have told you who it is for. Should you not be ashamed that a man of your position and of your means, son and heir to Lord Bethesda, should occupy a home meant for the aged and infirm and so keep your old gardener out of it?"

"Not a bit. Look here, Major Bennion, you talk of my means. I know most of the people here are old-age pensioners and thanks to you or your father they are very comfortably off but round the corner there are scores of houses, hundreds perhaps, with three or four wage-earners in the family who bring in twice as much in their pay packets as I get. I like living near my constituents and they like me to be here. It is handy for the House, just an easy run on the Underground."

"If you refuse to go," Roger said, "we might apply for an eviction order. That would test the validity of the tenancy."

"No doubt of its validity. But as I said, if anything more is due to you I am willing to pay it."

"Even the new Rent Act would not protect you and there may be other grounds for action."

"Such as?"

"Some of your neighbours suggest that the lady who is living with you is not your wife."

Ewen Jones laughed. "Because she writes and speaks as Gwennie Wren? That is just what they would suggest."

"Are they wrong? The question would of course be put to you when the case is heard. You can easily dispose of it by showing when and where you were married."

The M.P. still regarded him good-humouredly.

"Would it surprise you, Major Bennion, if two people, a man and a woman, having mutual interests and engaged in the same sort of work agreed to share a home? Would there be anything wrong in it?"

10

"I do not know what conclusion a Court would draw. My father designed these places, as I said, for the old and partially disabled. For two young and very able people, each earning a considerable income, to get possession of one of them would appear wrong to most people. It does to me."

"Assuming you were right, Gwennie Wren might not wish to marry me. We do not agree about everything. But we do agree that to have our incomes lumped together and so get lower allowances and a higher rate of tax would not be to our advantage."

"The law in that respect may be bad," Roger said. "If it is you are more responsible for it than we are. Do you think it would be good for you or your father if this came out in court?"

"I see your point," Ewen replied more seriously, "but do you see mine? It suits me to live here and I could not get alternative accommodation at anything like the same figure. Would it alter your views if Gwen left me?"

"That is your affair," Roger said. "We want the accommodation for Daniel Floss."

Ewen pondered for some moments.

"Look here, Bennion, suppose you spent a weekend at Welton Priory, my father's place—or rather, his wife's. You could see Floss and you could also see my father. You could put the case to him and you might suggest he should buy me a house or enable me to take a flat handy for Westminster."

"He makes you no allowance?"

"Not a farthing. His wife is a wealthy woman. She is not very fond of me and they think I ought to be able to manage. I can, living here, but not otherwise. If you, as an independent party, supported me it might help, especially as it would rid them of old Dan."

"How am I to be invited to Welton Priory?"

Ewen's smile returned. "Nothing easier, and it will give you a peep behind the scenes. In my view our party, call it Labour or Socialist as you like, wants pep. My father has agreed to my getting together in a fortnight's time at the Priory a Ginger Group to work out a plan of campaign. You could come then."

"Politics are not in my line," Roger said.

"So much the better. An independent view might be helpful. I am

11

quite serious about it and I hope it will do my father good. He was once called the Welsh Lion. He led two successful strikes. He was in the Cabinet but since he married this wealthy woman he has lost his fire. I would like to re-kindle it. If you are not interested in our talk, the grounds run down to the river and you might get some trout."

That, as it happened, was artful bait. Roger was a keen angler but Ruth, his wife, was not. It seemed selfish to indulge in the sport alone, especially as he was trying to interest her in golf. But she was shortly to take their infant, Penelope Ann, to visit her grandparents, the Dean and his wife, at Fenchester, and he was not going with them. It was a chance worth considering.

"Who will be in your party?" he asked.

"It is left to me. There will be a moderate houseful on Friday and on Sunday several more come over for the day. It is very hush-hush at present. It would not do for our party bosses to get wind of it. I would like to include a few non-politicians so that it shall not look suspicious. Do you know Captain and Mrs. Henshaw?"

"I think I have met them."

"They may come the day before. Of course Gwen will be there in her own right. Not a word to anybody, please of what we were saying just now. A few Trade Union M.P.s are bringing their wives and I hope to get Jeremiah along."

"Who is Jeremiah?" Roger asked.

"Don't you know him—old Tom Dayton? He always says Woe, woe and Doom. On Sunday there will be some of our heavy-weights."

"Sounds amusing. The Press?"

"Certainly not. Top-drawer secret. If anything leaked out you and the Henshaws would make it look like an ordinary house party. You could get a bit of fishing and you will see Floss and my father."

"Should not the invitation come from Lady Bethesda?"

"No. I just let them know who to expect and they fix it up. Good food and all the latest mod. con. You are not likely to see much of my worthy step-mother. She does not approve and she does not know who is coming, but she will not let us down. Too proud for that. She may spend most of her time with her son."

"She has a son—by your father?"

12

"Not a doubt of it! The precious Ambrose. A decent kid really; spoilt of course; about five years old. You will come?"

"I think I might manage it. But it makes no difference to my wanting this place."

"Good. I hope we shall arrange that you get it. Don't forget your rod."

3

Welton Priory

It is sometimes impossible to fix the precise impulses that govern our actions. We think we are free agents yet those actions may have results we were far from foreseeing. Is it possible that Fate—or Providence—spins a web much wider than we imagine and our choice is part of it?

Roger Bennion might have found it difficult to say exactly why he had accepted the rather odd invitation to visit Welton Priory. Ewen Jones had been fairly honest with him. He felt some liking for the fellow, though he was still determined to get him out of the house to which he should never have been admitted. The fact that Ruth and their infant were to be away for a time and the prospect of some fishing carried weight. It might be amusing to see a political plot in the making and he was always interested in genuine old buildings. All these things influenced him but it may be that Fate—or Providence—wanted him there for the part he was to play in the early but unexpected future. Whether or not fore-knowledge would have deterred him it is impossible to say. Those who know him best may think it would have whetted his appetite for the startling and sensational.

Having seen Ruth and Penelope Ann well on the way to Penchester he turned his car towards the Priory which was in that charming part of the country where Sussex joins Hampshire. The residence—which he had been told had been built earlier than Hampton Court Palace—appeared smaller than he had expected. The elevation was of mellowed red brick and had tall gables and lofty twisted chimneys. As he approached it through a long and well-kept drive, with glimpses of pretty flower garden on either side, it certainly looked attractive. He was to learn later it was larger than he had thought, though smaller than it once had been. Most mansions that have lasted for centuries have undergone changes. Many have been added to by succeeding owners, often with architectural crime and conglomerate hideousness.

The Priory, though reduced in size, retained much of its original charm. Shaped somewhat like the letter U it formed three sides of a quadrangle. The frontage was not great but the two wings continued for some depth, enclosing another, well kept flower garden. It would be expensive to maintain and what, had induced the millionaire brewer to acquire it and bequeath it to his daughter could only be surmised. But it was certainly a wonderful home for the former coal-miner, the one-time Lion of Wales.

It was about tea-time when Roger arrived, apparently a little earlier than he was expected. Contrary to Ewen's prediction he speedily made the acquaintance of Lady Bethesda. He was shown into a small room on the ground floor that was generally referred to as her ladyship's room. It could hardly be described as a model of good taste. The curtains and chair covers were of bright colours that would have offended a sensitive eye, and a few pieces of undoubtedly period furniture were alongside chairs of the metal tube design, comfortable but hardly in character.

He was interested rather than critical, and after a few moments his hostess entered leading a little boy by the hand.

"I am so pleased to meet you, Major Bennion," she said. "Ewen has gone to fetch some of his friends. He should be back soon. I am sorry my husband is not down yet. He has not been very well and has to reserve himself for what may be a late night. This is my son, Ambrose."

Roger bowed over the extended hand. Lady Bethesda was tall and thin. Not beautiful, but with dark eyes and straight black eyebrows. It was rather a hard face but he had the impression she could be pleasant when she tried—and she was trying.

As to Master Ambrose, he was a solemn-looking boy with dark eyes like his mother's. He was wearing black velvet knickers with a white silk shirt, something in the Fauntleroy style of a bygone age.

"You must tell me the games you play," Roger said to him genially. The boy offered a limp hand but made no reply.

14

"Tea will be here almost at once," Lady Bethesda remarked; "You will not mind if Ambrose has it with us? His nurse is out this afternoon."

"Nice and cosy," Roger smiled. "I had an idea Captain and Mrs. Henshaw might be here."

"They are. They came on Wednesday, but they went with Ewen. At least Sandra did. Her husband said he would try his luck fishing."

"I believe your stream is famous," Roger returned, "but perhaps you are more interested in politics, Lady Bethesda. With a husband so distinguished and with his son a Member of Parliament, you could hardly fail to be. Do you take an active part yourself?"

"I am afraid I do not. Frankly, politics bore me. Why cannot people be contented with things as they are instead of clamouring all the time for changes?"

"Then it is very good of you to allow this meeting in your beautiful home."

"I am not all that selfish. These things mean a lot to my husband, and it gives us a chance to see something of Ewen. He prefers to live in London."

Then the tea was wheeled in. Choice china, old silver and a profusion of cakes and sandwiches. It kept them busy for a time.

"You may be helping to make history," Roger remarked. "Do you know what Ewen's proposals will be?"

"I do not," was the rather acid reply. "He means well, I only hope he is not making mischief."

"Time will tell," Roger smiled. "History and mischief have always been intertwined."

They chatted for some time. He asked questions about the old abbey but she replied very briefly, attending more to the little boy, telling him what cakes he might take. He was certainly well behaved and did not clamour for what was denied him. Then the footman who had brought in the tea returned and whispered that someone wanted her ladyship on the telephone.

"How annoying," she said. "Will you excuse me, Major Bennion? I am sure Ambrose will be safe with you. He has finished his tea."

"Quite safe. Have you finished?" he asked as she left the room.

"Mum said so," was the reply.

"And Mummies always know, don't they?" It was not for him to undermine authority, even with the chocolate eclair at which the boy looked rather longingly. "Tell me, Ambrose, about the games you play?"

"My father is a lord."

"I know, but that doesn't prevent you having a bit of fun sometimes, does it Are there any little boys in the village you can play with?"

The big, rather expressionless eyes looked at him. "My father is a lord," was again the reply.

"I have a little girl. She is younger than you but she is full of mischief. Don't you ever want to get into mischief? I know your father is a lord," he added to forestall the reply, "but wouldn't you like to throw stones or climb a tree sometimes?"

"Brigid wouldn't let me."

"Brigid is your nurse? What games do you play with her?"

"Snakes 'n' ladders.' She reads to me. I've got a pony."

"Good. Can it run fast or jump?"

"Brigid gen'rally leads him."

"Do you ever get your clothes in a mess?" He shook his head.

"Have you any friends?"

"Rhoda said she was my friend."

"Good. Is Rhoda a little girl about your age?"

Another shake of the head. "She's growed up."

"That is a pity. What would happen if you did mess your clothes and were naughty?"

"I'd be put in bed till it was time to be dressed again."

"Not smacked?"

"Mummie said no one mustn't touch me. My father is a lord."

"What exactly is a lord?" Roger was almost impatient.

"My father is. Everyone obeys him."

16

At that moment, rather to his relief, the mother returned.

"That tiresome Mr. Ruttle," she said. "Something wrong with his car. He will be an hour late. What would you like to do?"

"Don't let me be in the way. If I may I will get my rod and find my way to the river. I may meet Henshaw."

"You cannot miss your way. Cross the lawn and the path leads straight to it."

"Thank you. Do you fish?"

"No. I think it cruel."

"But you eat fish?"

"Certainly I do if it is caught in a net, not with a hook in its mouth."

"That is a point of view," Roger said. "I have seen the boats coming in loaded with gasping fish. I almost believe they would prefer to be hooked and despatched quickly."

She did not deign to argue. "The maid will show you your room," she said. "Come, Ambrose."

Roger soon fetched his tackle and made his way to the stream. The lawn, as Lady Bethesda had called it, stretched for almost the entire width of the property. At one time the village cricket matches had been played there but her ladyship had discontinued the practice after the arrival of her son.

As he crossed it Roger felt he had not made too good an impression on his hostess. After all, it was the promise of fishing that had brought him there, though she probably was not aware of the fact. She might be a very humane woman but she was certainly narrow-minded. He was more interested in her son. She was hardly fitting him to play his part in the world. A nicely mannered little boy, but too much cotton wool is bad for anyone. Things might be better when he went to school—if she could find a school fit for him to go to!

At the far end of the lawn, between the trees, was the broad pathway leading to the river. Near the river but inside the garden was a wooden hut used perhaps by bathers as a changing room. At the side of the hut he saw a young couple in a very loving attitude. Was the girl the absent nurse or were they both members of the house party? He paused for a moment. Although they were holding each others' arms they did not appear to be talking or expressing affection. They had a tense look as though listening to something.

He coughed and took a step forward. The girl heard him and at once turned away. The young man followed her and they were lost in the bushes that apparently bordered the stream.

He went on. As he did so the door of the hut opened and two other people looking rather angry came out.

"Captain Henshaw?" Roger said, going forward. "Lady Bethesda told me you were trying your luck. I thought I would have a cast."

"May your luck be better than mine," was the terse reply. "Nothing doing."

"How are you, Mrs. Henshaw?" Roger smiled to the young woman. "Lady Bethesda thought you had gone with Ewen to pick up some of his friends."

"She should have done," Oswald said. "Then I might have caught something."

"More perhaps than you expected," Sandra remarked. "Ewen's car is small; there might not have been room enough."

"He is expected back soon," Roger said. "I think I will look round and see if fortune is kind."

They did not encourage conversation. He walked on. Beyond the hut was a gate opening on to a footpath beside the stream. It looked inviting but his luck was no better than Henshaw's.

4

The Ginger Group

Cocktails were served before dinner. All the guests, including Mr. Ruttle, had arrived. Roger was greeted by Ewen and introduced to his fellow M.P.s. There appeared to be seven of them. He had heard there was a new aristocracy in the Labour party, the Intelligentsia as opposed to the Horny-handed, the public school class in distinction from those who had got their start in the mines, the railways or the factories. Of the former Hugh Gaitskell and his predecessor Lord Attlee stood pre-eminent. Of the latter he thought of Keir Hardie, I. H. Thomas Bevin, Nye Bevan and many others. The more credit to those who from humble beginnings had risen by their own efforts and personality to the highest rank.

Of the men he now met the only one whose name was known to him was Bill Ruttle, whose car mishap had so annoyed Lady Bethesda. He was big in build, loud in voice and self-assured. He had often been in trouble with the Speaker in the House of Commons. He had been "named" on more than one occasion. To be named is not to be famed, but it may be a short road to notoriety.

The one of the group who might have belonged to the intelligentsia was introduced as Fred Gibbons. He appeared more cultured, quieter and with some sense of humour. Roger was no active partisan but if there was mischief brewing it might be interesting to hear what it was.

He was not introduced to their ladies, mostly stout and middle-aged, who formed another group by themselves. He was how ever surprised to see among them the young girl he had disturbed beside the hut. He could not identify her companion. She and the Henshaw were helping to circulate drinks.

As soon as he could Roger went to Lord and Lady Bethesda, who were a little apart from their guests. She introduced him to her husband and then moved away. Roger remembered the Welsh Lion as he had been in his stormier days. Then his hair had been dark like his son Ewen's. It was now almost white. He had in some way shrunk. He looked a sick man.

"Years ago I attended one of your rallies in Trafalgar Square," Roger said to him. "Things have changed a bit since then."

"There is still room for improvement," the old man replied.

"How horrible if there were not! The thought of a world where any change must be for the worse is quite frightening. It is good of you to let your son and his friends put us on the right road."

"Provided it is the left road."

"You travel with him?" Roger asked.

"I don't know yet where he is going. There can be a smash if

19

you travel too fast in any direction. Have you seen my boy Ambrose?"

It was an abrupt question. Roger gathered his lordship did not want to commit himself on any line in politics.

"I have. A nice little chap; not a lion cub yet, but there is no knowing what he may become."

Then they were joined by Sandra Henshaw and Ewen.

"Dad," said the latter, "we want you to settle a bet. When did women first get the vote and who was Prime Minister at the time? Sandra says women are naturally more conservative than men."

"Female Suffrage," Lord Bethesda replied. "That brings back memories of those marvellous people Mrs. Pankhurst and her daughters Christabel and Sylvia. But I doubt if one woman in ten who now have the vote know even their names. Very clever and determined they were. I was once at a meeting addressed by Christabel. She was telling her audience what her mother and her friends were suffering for the cause they believed in; imprisonment, forcible feeding and every kind of indignity. 'Two of us,' she said, 'hid in the House of Commons for twenty-four hours without food or water so that when proceedings started they might shout our slogan Votes for Women. How many of you men would have the pluck and endurance to do a thing like that?' A heckler shouted, 'We do not go where we are not wanted.' Christabel replied in a flash. 'I am glad you were so sure of your welcome tonight!' There was a roar of laughter and the heckler shut up."

"A very smart retort," Roger said.

"Very," Ewen agreed, "but what is the answer to our problem?"

"Memories are short," his father replied. "Women got the vote in 1918 and Lloyd George was Prime Minister. It was an agreed measure as women had done such splendid work in the war. I should say most women vote as their husbands tell them—but an increase in the price of eggs will always be more important to them than foreign policy."

"Quite right, too," said Sandra. "Thank you, Lord Bethesda. I lose my bet but I am at least right in that."

"I hope the loss is not a heavy one," Roger smiled.

"Purely a question of currency," Ewen smirked, looking at Sandra, who cast down her eyes.

Then dinner was announced and they went into what had no doubt been the refectory room in former days. There were twenty of them in all and the table was a noble sight with gay flowers, burnished silver and sparkling glass. The food was equally stimulating. Roger guessed Lady Bethesda was responsible for it and wondered why she had not thought plainer fare sufficient for the company. No doubt she had her reasons. He had noticed before that the men did most of the talking and their wives, unused to such grandeur, had grouped together to whisper among themselves. Now the attention of all was devoted to what was placed before them. It was a demonstration of what a Labour leader might achieve if he married wealth, but its wisdom was open to question. Four menservants did the waiting and did it well.

Roger found himself next to a Mrs. Doodell whose husband was a Trade Union M.P. She was not talkative and he was glad to turn to the girl on his left, none other than the one he had seen outside the hut. He noticed that Ewen and Sandra were opposite to them and seemed to be getting on very well. The dress of the ladies was somewhat remarkable, as while three or four wore dark clothes almost up to their chins, others went to the further extreme and showed their breeding by a display of bosom that would have satisfied a film star. Lady Bethesda had a pale green sleeveless frock doing justice to her necklace and bracelet of diamonds and emeralds.

The attire of the men was equally varied. Lord Bethesda wore a dinner jacket suit, as did Roger Bennion, Oswald Henshaw and Fred Gibbons. The others were in ordinary dark clothes or tweeds, perhaps to show their democratic convictions or maybe the limitations of their wardrobes. Ewen had been in two minds in the matter. He had at first kept to his day suit, thinking it would be more in character with the part he had to play and might possibly save some of his guests from embarrassment. Then he had seen Sandra in a lovely off-the-shoulder blue frock that toned well with her beautiful eyes. He decided he could not sit beside her as he was and had dashed off hastily to change into a suit like his father's.

"Nobody yet has told me who you are," Roger remarked to his younger neighbour. "You do not look like an earnest orator, but I may be wrong. Are you so famous that I ought to know?"

She turned and smiled at him. A very charming smile. She had red hair, green eyes and pleasing features. She wore a simple frock of primrose yellow with a single string of pearls. Her hands were good and had no rings.

"It is rather tempting to tell you something wonderful about myself; or to hint at something mysterious," she said in a sweet voice with a musical little laugh, "but you would soon find out the truth. I am Rhoda Rees."

"That does not convey a great deal, except that you are a friend of Master Ambrose whose father is a lord."

"Who told you that?" she asked quickly.

"He did. Are you in any way responsible for his upbringing?"

"I am not. He is a dear little boy really, but—I had better not say what I think. I am the niece of the lord, the daughter of his sister, and also his secretary. I help Aunt Connie in somethings but not with Ambrose. I might have a bad influence! He has a maid and a nursery governess who bring him up in the way his mother thinks he should go."

"Poor little devil," Roger murmured. "It may be better when he goes to school. Does his father approve of it all?"

"I don't think he does. Aunt Connie is devoted to him but she won't let him grow up naturally."

"I gathered that she approves of you?"

"Not whole-heartedly."

"What a shame! There is something else I know about you, Rhoda—if I may call you that."

"What is it?"

"If I were a fortune teller I should say there was a tall dark man in your life—"

"So you saw us!" she flushed. "You are very inquisitive. I don't think I like you."

She turned away and Roger caught a remark from his other neighbour who was mopping up some gravy with a piece of bread. She was a buxom woman somewhat like a famous and popular M.P. from Liverpool, though not built on quite such generous lines.

"Jolly good, this stew," she was saying. "I'm a fair hand at a stew myself; though Mr. Doodell likes something he can get his teeth into." From her speech she was a Londoner.

22

It figured on the menu as Ris de veau Mercelle, a delicious compound of sweetbreads, mushrooms and other things. Roger beckoned the waiter who brought her a further portion.

"Do you help your husband in his constituency?" he asked.

"I do my best, but I ain't a speaker like what he is. At election times I call on the women and ask 'em what they want. When they tell me I say vote for my husband and you'll get it. Generally it's more pay and cheaper food."

"If everyone got more money, food and everything else would be dearer, wouldn't they?" Roger asked.

"I don't argue," Mrs. Doodell said, "I just tell 'em."

"Fair enough," Roger smiled. "Where is your husband's constituency?"

"North London. Lived there all our lives; we both have. Boy and girl sweet'earts as you may say. Never wanted no one else. I always encouraged him going to his night classes. See how he's got on, as good as any of 'em. It was a Tory strong'old once but never since they got my Bert."

A sincere tribute if not an impartial one. Having delivered it she attacked the food. Rhoda in the meantime had found her further neighbour, a Mr. Edmonds, deep in a political argument across the table. So she turned back to Roger.

"I am sorry," she said, "but I ought to have asked if you found Brother Gregory's room comfortable?"

"Who may Brother Gregory be?" he asked.

"The monk whose cell has been allotted to you. All the rooms in that wing were originally occupied by the brothers. The Prior had good rooms in the front which my uncle and aunt now use. Of course there have been a lot of alterations through the ages and Aunt Connie's father threw two cells into one, but they are still quite small. All are the same on that passage."

"So I may be displacing Thomas as well as Gregory?"

"Do you mind?"

"Not provided the bed is a little softer than those holy men fancied."

"I can promise that," she laughed. "My uncle does not often entertain. We tried to give decent rooms to the married couples but single men like you, and of course, Ewen, have to be content with the cells."

"I cannot claim to be a single man, but the room is very adequate for one who deserts his wife, even for a weekend. How are you quartered?"

"I have a very nice room but I gave it to Mr. and Mrs. Boyne. Don't let them know! Even then we should have been rather puzzled but Captain and Mrs. Henshaw offered to take two little rooms—plenty of them—and that gave another big one."

"Where do you put the crowd that is to come on Sunday?"

"There will be about thirty of them, but only for lunch. We can manage that."

"Housekeeping is more of an art than I realised. Do you always live in this style, with these faithful servitors?"

"Good heavens, no! We have two who live in and the gardener's wife sometimes, and some help from the village. On special occasions like this Aunt Connie borrows from one of her hotels."

"Lucky Aunt Connie! Tell me, Rhoda, who is the dark handsome young woman on your uncle's right?"

"You ought to know her. Her photograph is often in the papers. She is Gwennie Wren. She writes a lot and speaks, too. Ewen thinks her marvellous."

"Is she also in a cell? Or have you underground dungeons for women who talk?"

She laughed. "She has quite a nice cell not far from yours. There are queer places below though we do not use them. There are the Little Ease we sometimes show people."

"A cell where one can neither stand up nor lie down?"

"Yes. They had some nice ideas, hadn't they? I suppose it was a punishment or penance. I sometimes wonder how they endured it. I suppose we are getting softer. We take the greatest care of our athletes yet they are continually crocking up. Those people lived for years in damp cells and often had a bit of torture, too. How do you account for it?"

"It does seem odd," Roger said, "but you must remember Brothers Gregory and Thomas were content to hobble about their duties. They were not called on to run a hundred yards in under ten seconds or play football and cricket against champions. You have not yet told me about the ghost."

"We haven't got one."

"No ghost? A place of this age, with underground torture chambers and no ghost? How do you account for mysterious noises at night?"

"Are you trying to frighten me? I don't hear them. If I did I'd say to myself we must get the rat man again."

"You are a girl with strong nerves. You were not vexed with me for seeing you this afternoon, were you? It was not really my fault."

She again gave that charming blush. "I suppose not. Can you keep a secret?"

"The oyster is a chatterbox compared with me."

"Then I'll risk it. Jeremy Valiance and I are engaged, but are not supposed to be."

"Why not?"

"Aunt Connie does not approve. She says if I wait a bit she will find me someone worthy of Lord Bethesda's niece."

"The son of another lord?"

"Something like that, but I only want Jeremy. She says he must not come to the house so I have to meet him in the garden when I can."

"What does your uncle think about it?"

"He leaves it to Aunt Connie."

"What does Jeremy do? Are you dependent on your aunt and uncle?"

"Jerry is the village schoolmaster and they are on the committee that runs these things. If they knew about us they might get him transferred to the other side of the county. We don't want that. I am over twenty-one but Aunt Connie says she will give me a dowry when I marry the right man. Jerry and I are saving as hard as we can and when we have a certain amount we shall just marry and tell them afterwards."

"Jerry is a lucky fellow. Have they anything against him except that he has no blue blood?"

"We haven't blue blood either, only coal dust! Uncle was a miner and my mother married a miner. I don't pretend to be what I am

25

not. Uncle Jim helped me to get a decent education and that is how I met Jerry. He says Uncle Jim was a grand chap before he married Aunt Connie, but now she is poisoning him with riches!"

"Many people would consider it a very slow poison and a pleasant one," Roger said, "but I see his point. How do you get on with cousin Ewen?"

"He is all right. He likes Jerry but we have not told him. Aunt Connie does not really approve of Ewen either."

"Do you know where he lives?"

"Somewhere in the East End of London, in his constituency. He once said it was called Old Nick's Folly."

"Old Nick being my father—"

"Oh—I am sorry Rhoda murmured. "I never thought—"

"Why should you? I came here to try to get Ewen to clear out. Do you not think Aunt Connie might help him to move to a neighbourhood more worthy of the family?"

"She might," Rhoda said doubtfully.

"My father's folly was perhaps the finest thing he has done. He built those houses for deserving old people. Ewen got his by a sort of mistake. Now we want it for Dan Floss, your gardener."

"How splendid. Ewen ought to go at once."

"He says he cannot afford to unless the parents help. That is why I am here. Will you speak a word if you get a chance?"

"Of course I will."

"Good, and if I can help you and Jerry you may rely on me. Do you know Gwennie Wren pretty well?"

"Not really. Ewen thinks a lot of her."

"Are they likely to marry?"

"He seems in no hurry."

"More interested at the moment in Sandra Henshaw?"

"I don't know. She is very pretty, isn't she? I like her but I do not care much for her husband."

"I met them as I passed that hut," Roger said, changing the subject. "Are there good fish in the stream?"

"I believe so."

"I did not get a bite. I thought perhaps they had all been caught for us to eat tonight." They were tackling roast duck at the moment.

"Why so?" Rhoda asked.

"Friday at the Priory. I am sure Brother Gregory would have been busy with rod and line. His only chance of supper."

"I am afraid that is one of the customs we do not observe," she laughed.

"Perhaps the fish are specially wary on Fridays. Is the fishing free?"

"No. It is ours for quite a stretch. When Mr. Marden, that is, Aunt Connie's father, first came he wanted to close the footpath, too. There was a bit of trouble about it and he had to give way."

"Did not make for popularity?"

"He didn't understand the village people. Of course newcomers are always regarded as foreigners for a generation or two."

"How did they take to your uncle?"

"He does his best to be friendly with them."

A little later, when all had eaten and drunk well, that uncle at the head of the table rapped on it with his knife and everyone turned towards him.

"As you know," he said, "my son Ewen thinks, rightly or wrongly, that our Party needs a more progressive policy if we are to win the next election. He says we want a Ginger Group and hopes he can get our leaders to adopt his views. I think it would be a good thing if he told us tonight what these views are; a sort of agenda. Then you can consider and discuss them among yourselves tomorrow and be prepared to say at the bigger meeting on Sunday how far you support them. He has only given me a vague outline but I am sure you will listen carefully to what he proposes."

There was none of the old roar about the Lion's speech. He spoke slowly and clearly and to Roger, at any rate, he was committing himself to nothing. There was a burst of applause which was renewed when Ewen rose to his feet.

"Would the ladies prefer to withdraw?" he asked. "They may find it dull."

"They are as much concerned as the men," Gwennie Wren said loudly. "They have votes and they pay taxes."

"And 'ave to run the 'omes," added Mrs. Doodell, to more applause.

5

The Programme

"It is very good of my father and Lady Bethesda to have given us this opportunity of getting together to settle some of our problems. I think we can agree on that if on nothing else."

Ewen smiled, and there was again a ripple of approval. He was a fine-looking man and his big voice boomed through the lofty rooms. Sandra sitting beside him clapped her little hands.

"I should like to make it clear I am speaking only for myself. Some of you are aware to some extent of what I have in mind, but I do not want anyone to be victimised because they have listened to me. I hope however before we have finished I shall persuade some if not all of you that what I say is right. I will be as brief as I can though there is a lot of ground to cover.

"The first point is this: Are we a Labour Party or a Socialist Party? Sometimes one name is used, sometimes the other, but the two are very different. I say we should declare boldly and clearly that we are a Socialist Party and should build our programme accordingly."

"Hear, hear," rumbled round the room.

"I can find a simple illustration of what I mean. Our late leader, whom we all greatly respected, retired was awarded an hereditary earldom with a pension I believe of two thousand a year. That was all right in a Labour Party but all wrong in a Socialist one."

There was less applause at this.

"I will return to that later. My next point is that the worker must rule but the worker must work. Socialism is not a plan by which the drones eat all the honey. There are drones in every section of

28

society, from the capitalists who put money but no effort into work, to the shirkers who seek to do as little as possible and to get more than they should for it. We must fight them all. We must stop these little strikes that do no good to anyone except the foreigner who is waiting eagerly to collar our markets."

Doubt showed in some faces. "The Unions won't stand for that," Bill Ruttle cried with some emphasis. He was a burly man and had an aggressive way of speaking.

"Don't misunderstand me," Ewen went on. "I am not against the Unions. I want to see them more powerful but we must not let little sections cause stoppages over trifles. A Union must seek the good of all. I am strongly in favour of equality of opportunity but there must also be equality of responsibility."

"What d'you mean by that?" someone asked.

"I will soon tell you. I favour more Unions and smaller Unions so that they may be closer to the workers. There should of course be the Regional Councils but I would like to see a Grand Council and only that Grand Council should be able to call a strike. Think what that would mean! The local Union that has a grievance reports it to the Regional Council. If they cannot settle it, it passes to the Grand Council. If the Grand Council consider it right they call on the employers or the commissioners or whoever is concerned to do what they demand. If this is not done they call a strike—not of one trade but of every trade! It is a standstill for the whole country. Nothing and nobody could resist it!"

He paused and there was some commotion. One or two seemed to support the idea, some called it impossible. "A steam hammer to crack a monkey nut," someone remarked.

"The Grand Council would not call a strike over trifles," Ewen said.

"How long would this Grand Council take to act?" asked Gibbons, a stout little man from an East London constituency. "My men won't wait. They want action."

"It would end strikes," declared Edmonds, a friend of Ewen's. "The Council would fix a wage structure taking due account of the cost of living and of foreign competition. Everyone would be better off in the long run."

"Sounds like Russia to me," muttered Ted Boyne.

29

"Aye," said Ruttle. "Who would be on this Grand Council and who would be the Stalin or Kruschev at the head of it?"

Ewen waved a hand.

"It would be quite unlike Russia. The Soviet has practically abolished Trade Unions. We should be all for them. We should have freedom of speech, a free Press and free elections. Russia has none of these things. They may be on the way but the way is long and slow. Our Grand Council would be elected by the workers, not appointed by anyone."

"What about the Chief?" Ruttle asked.

"Of course there must be a chairman or chief; he would be no Stalin. Stalin has been debunked by his own people but the dictator system remains. Our chairman would be no dictator but a man of cool judgment, respected by all. I have in mind one who could admirably fill the post and give us a good start. His work for the toiling masses is well known and his sense of justice and fair play are recognised everywhere. If he has some means he would be able to help us in the early days before we were established. Need I say I allude to my father?"

There were murmurs of approval, hesitant and polite rather than enthusiastic. Roger saw Lady Bethesda frowning angrily at her stepson, but that was unnecessary. Her husband held up his hand to check the applause.

"Not me, Ewen," he said. "You will want a younger man. Yourself if you like, but not me."

"The question hardly arises," Ewen smiled, "but someone asked it. The point I am getting at is this. We want work to be regarded from a new angle. As you know, even if we do not all acknowledge it, the worker today in many cases has no heart in his job. He couldn't care less. We must change that; we want him to have pride in his work as his fathers and grandfathers did. There are somethings we can learn from America."

"What?" a voice asked.

"I will tell you. The miners there have their own pension fund and it does not cost them a penny. In one year they paid out 127 million dollars in pensions, medical care and other benefits, and they have a reserve of more than that. How is it got? Nearly half a dollar is a first charge on every ton of coal mined. The Unions therefore have a direct interest in increasing production. They are proud of it. It is in part due to more mechanisation but the welfare fund takes care of those who lose their jobs. We want something like that."

"Are there no strikes in America?" Gibbons asked.

"Of course there are, but not a lot of silly petty ones. Their welfare leaves them free to negotiate wage claims."

"No strikes means slavery," Gibbons declared.

Ewen disregarded him. "In a Socialist state as I see it the individual works not only for himself and not for the boss but for all his fellows and for his country. As Edmonds said, it means greater benefit for everyone."

"Co-partnership," Mr. Doodell suggested.

"Yes and no," Ewen replied. "Co-partnership is definitely anti-labour. Some concerns make bigger profits than others, therefore the workers in one concern, perhaps because it has a lower capital, would receive in wages and profits much more than others doing precisely the same job in another and similar concern. Nothing would be more certain to produce discontent. Certainly no one would want to share losses. As I see it the Grand Council would fix the wage, a higher figure I hope than at present. But they would also fix a ceiling for dividends. All earnings above the profit necessary to pay that dividend would be pooled for the national benefit, for the good of all. In every public company one or more of the directors would be elected by the workers so that their interests were safeguarded."

This received more applause than before, though there were some dubious shakes of the head and Lady Bethesda looked definitely displeased.

"How that pool would be allocated is not for me to say. I am no specialist in these matters. If the ceiling for dividends were fixed at, let us say, ten per cent, the pool, taking everything above that figure, would soon run into many millions. Countless commercial concerns pay from fifteen to twenty per cent and quite a number up to eighty or a hundred per cent. That excess could be used to reduce taxation or still better, as I hope to show, to pay off our National Debt. We cannot for ever continue to pay interest on the thousands of millions we spent on the wars.

"Some may object that this would be a form of capital levy and would fall on one section of the community only. Also that the large dividends do not represent the return to the share holder, some of

31

whom paid three or four pounds for a five-shilling share. I recognise the difficulty but it is not a capital levy. The shareholders retain their capital and after a time when our economic position has re-established itself the old dividends, in whole or in part, might be resumed.

"This brings me to what I will call our Five Years' Plan. Of course we have read and we accept the official pronouncements of our Party. One journalist described them as a thorough analysis of the obvious interlaced with a lot of long-hairy theory. We want actions not words!"

He paused and was rewarded with some mild "Hear, hears."

"Not all people are shareholders of public companies are shareholders of public companiesto all wealthy persons as well as to workers and the Unions. During the five years all estates of over ten thousand pounds should be valued for death duties and one half the death duty should be paid during that term and credit given for it when death occurs. But death makes one think of the Statute of Mortmain. Are you familiar with that?"

"Tell us," Gibbons said, perhaps a little scornfully.

"The first Statute of Mortmain was in the reign of Henry III. It was to deal with lands held by a corporation or dead hand so that the Crown or others might be deprived of the incidents of seignery. It has been amended from time to time but we still find enormous estates held by the Church, by corporations and city guilds, by the universities, Trade Unions and other such bodies No death duties are payable on them nor is any income tax charged. A wealthy man may pay tax up to 8/6 in the £. These, rich concerns pay only the statutory rate of 8/6. Is that fair?"

"No! No!" said several voices.

"Their funds support charities," Gibbons remarked.

"I would set up a commission to see what they could fairly be charged during the five years and I think a vast sum would be realised. You may ask and rightly ask what is the purpose of the collection of this enormous amount of money. I can tell you in a word. It is to pay off or very greatly reduce our incredible load of debt."

"Wants a lot of thinking about, that do," Bill Ruttle muttered.

"It does," Ewen agreed. "You must remember that so far no party has made any real endeavour to reduce or wipe out our nation's debts. All they do is to urge us to save, or in other words to add to our debt, for the savings have to be repaid. It is in fact pure inflation. Reduction of debt must be our priority number one. Statistics are dull things and I am not particularly good at them, but from the best sources available I gather our National Debt is now over twenty-seven thousand million pounds. We can hardly understand such astronomical figures. Recently we were adding about a million pounds a day to our debt. The interest on it and the expenses of dealing with it cost nearly two millions a day. Yet nobody does anything to cut it. When we do that the reduction of taxation will fellow."

"Who will live to see it?" Gwennie Wren asked.

"All of us, I hope. It will not be easy, it may not be pleasant, but self-denial is not thinking what the other fellow can do without; it is willingness to bear our share. Twenty-seven thousand million pounds! Can you realise it? If you could pay off five pounds a second in every hour of the twenty-four, day and night, it would take a hundred and seventy years to meet it."

"Do I understand our workers must wait a hundred and seventy years for their benefit?" Gibbons asked. "Some of them, at any rate the older ones, might get impatient."

Ewen was irritated at the laughter that followed.

"The benefits would start the moment we got the power to enforce them," he said. "My illustration was only to show to the meanest intelligence, including Fred Gibbons's, the magnitude of the task. The dividend limit would reduce the cost of living enormously and at once. The prices of most things would topple as the incentive of gain disappeared. That would benefit everyone."

"Then what happens to your pool?" Ruttle queried. "You cannot have it both ways."

"Oh, yes, you can! The companies would want to maintain their output and would realise the benefits debt reduction would bring. Let me remind you that when the Tories proposed the issue of Premium Bonds some of the bishops and many of our own people opposed them. They swallowed the camel of football pools by which millions lose money every week and strained at the gnat of these bonds by which no one loses anything. What they did not see was that all such bonds add to our debt and make real recovery more difficult. The crazy thing is that if you draw £1,000 or one of the other prizes the Government still owes your original pound. In theory a man might draw £1,000 a month for the rest of his life and still be entitled to have his pound back! Debt reduction is our first duty. Then the British pound will return to something like its old value."

6

More Ginger

Roger had been listening to all that was said and had watched the faces of the hearers. Two or three seemed willing to back Ewen in all he proposed; a few were definitely hostile; more appeared to foresee trouble with the Unions and would not commit themselves to that. The women for the most part were bored. They had enjoyed a good dinner and would have liked to take off their shoes and go to sleep.

Such was not the case with Gwennie Wren. She was watching Ewen closely and had made some angry comments. Had they quarrelled? Did she know she was to be ejected from the house she had shared with him? Sandra gave every appearance of being interested, in all Ewen said. She generally murmured "Hear, hear" when others did. Ossie, her husband, made no such pretence. Half the time his eyes were closed.

Coffee had been served and cigars and cigarettes handed round. Some of the men preferred their pipes. Gwen took a cigar, but she soon allowed it to go out. Lord Bethesda was attentive but gave no indication of his feelings. There was no doubt of his wife's disapproval.

"Enjoying it?" Roger asked softly of his neighbour.

Not much," Rhoda replied. "I have heard most of it before. I doubt if they will ever agree."

"So much for our main object," Ewen was saying. "We want to be free of debt as soon as we can and our appalling taxation will disappear. Some may think with such vast realisations of property we shall all be sellers and value will vanish. How wrong they are! The money will not go up in smoke as it does in war. It will be paid

34

to the bondholders who will have to re-invest it. So there will be as many buyers as sellers. We shall be cutting out dead wood. I foresee such a boom in business as we have seldom if ever known before."

There was some applause, though Dayton murmured, "I wonder," and Ruttle muttered, "Dream-land!"

"Anyway let us leave that and return to something I mentioned before. All hereditary titles must be abolished. I was talking recently to one of our peers and he told me his title dated back to the Conquest. Why should I bow down to him and call him My Lord because of something done by a remote ancestor nearly a thousand years ago? In every reign since then men have been created dukes, earls, viscounts and barons because they did good work for the nation or assisted in the amours of the King. I say they must all go. The older the title the further off the good works that occasioned it and the greater the reason for discontinuing it."

His voice boomed more loudly and the applause was more sustained, though some looked a little doubtfully at their lordly host.

"I am at least disinterested in this," Ewen resumed with a smile. "It would wipe out any chance of my becoming a peer, but why not? Do not think I am opposed to titles. Quite the reverse. If a man renders exemplary service to his country by all means give him a title to show appreciation of his work But why should his son or his brother or his cousin, who may have done nothing for the public weal, inherit that title? Earl Attlee by all means, but why a line of Earl Attlees, unless they earn the honour? In our Church the most eminent churchman may become an archbishop but his son is not an archbishop or even a rural dean. He is a plain mister unless he also merits some distinction. What is good enough for the Church should be good enough for us!"

The "Hear hears!" were loud. Bill Ruttle asked, "What about the House of Lords?"

"That, of course, must go. I believe in a second chamber but it must be on a democratic basis. We know what the Tories propose but it does not go far enough. I suggest each county council should appoint a member to the Senate. Each university should do the same. The Trade Unions might nominate a certain number. Every profession, medical, legal, scientific, and the stage should be represented. Each Church should have a member. It would be an assembly of the finest brains in the country. The outgoing lords like

35

everyone else would be entitled to stand for election to either House should they wish to do so."

"What of the Royal Family?" Gwennie Wren asked.

"A Socialist State and a Monarchy are contradictions in terms. I yield to none in my admiration for our beautiful young Queen. She and her husband have done more than seemed possible for the cause they represent."

"She and her family are the most popular people in the land," Gwennie asserted. "The Crown is the symbol of unity throughout the Commonwealth."

"They give good copy to the Press," Ewen said dryly. "Suppose the heir to the throne had been a fat and foolish woman like Queen Anne, would the cause of Royalty have been so popular? Perhaps you remember Lander—

'George the First was always reckoned Vile, but viler George the Second, And what mortal ever heard Any good of George the Third? When from earth the Fourth descended (God be Praised!) the Georges ended.'"

"The writer of these lines was, of course, wrong. The next King was tolerantly known as Silly Billy. Queen Victoria did much to restore the prestige of the Royal House and we can agree that George the Fifth and George the Sixth played their parts well. But as to the Crown being a symbol of unity, what of Ireland and India and Ceylon? What of the countries all over the world that are clamouring for independence? Canada, Australia and New Zealand acknowledge the Queen but they are independent nevertheless. They would still be our kith and kin when Royalty ceased. I say Monarchy must go."

"I pity the party that went to the country with such a cry," Gwennie declared.

"If we are Socialists we must nail our colours to the mast," Ewen retorted. "Mind you, I did not say the Queen should be deposed. I only object to the hereditary principle. Elizabeth the Second might be our greatest Monarch but she would be the last."

At this several people started talking at once. There were exchanges across the table in which some of the women joined. The Queen meant a good deal to them and so did her young children. They also got on to the subject of Princess Margaret. After a time Lord Bethesda rapped on the table for silence.

"Have you anything else to say, Ewen?" he asked.

"I might talk all night," his son replied, with a smile. "Much might be said about Zeta but you would probably not understand what I was saying and neither should I myself."

"Hear, hear," and some laughter followed.

"It is hoped that in twenty years Zeta will transform the world. That and the conquest of space are problems for the scientists. They should not be party matters. If possible they should be under international control, provided always that Britain, the pioneer, be not squeezed out by bigger and wealthier states. Our first step should be to strengthen our finances in the way I have suggested. Then we shall be able worthily to play our part and the bogey fear of war may disappear."

This was applauded. He continued: "There is the immediate foreign policy. Has our Party a foreign policy?"

"What of the United Nations?" Doodell enquired.

"Which are the united nations?" Ewen retorted. "If they formed an impartial tribunal their influence would be enormous. But they do not. Was Russia deterred by their opinions when it let loose its tanks in Budapest? The so-called organisation is split into three or four groups which bargain with each other to get their own ends, irrespective of the merits of a case. In the Suez affair our party was arm in arm with Russia. There must be something wrong when that can happen. But we are not concerned with that tonight. My programme will amend some of our marriage laws. I would certainly disestablish the Church—"

"And dis-endow it?" someone asked.

"Not entirely. I would appoint a commission to examine its endowments. Those made specifically to the Church of England would remain its property. Those made to the Church of Rome prior to the Reformation would be forfeited. The Non-Conformist Churches have to pay their own ministers, why should not the Church of England? When we are rid of our terrible millstone of debt, or have greatly reduced it, together with the two million pounds a day it costs to administer, our opportunities for good will be almost incalculable. Better schools, more pay for teachers, increased wages for all the Services including the police, improved prisons and better conditions for the prison staffs—but I have said enough. As my father pointed out we have all tomorrow to think

37

things over. Then on Sunday when our friends join us we shall know what we have to tell them."

There was a generous meed of applause when he sat down. Before it subsided Gwennie Wren was on her feet. She was handsome, though not a beauty. Her black hair and eyebrows and her dark eyes showed her as a strong and intelligent woman.

"I would like Ewen to answer one question," she said. "He has talked of a Ginger Group to rouse the party to more forceful action. Does he or does he not wish to win the next election?"

"I most certainly do," Ewen replied.

"Then you are going the wrong way about it. To unite against us all who are loyal to the Crown, to the Church, and to the present Trades Unions is to ask for the biggest defeat in our history. It is madness."

"I agree with Gwennie," Bill Ruttle declared. "The Unions have done and are doing splendid work. They will not consent to be under a Grand Council that can overrule their decisions—even if he is the chairman!"

Then it was Fred Gibbons's turn; He stood up and spoke with an easy smile.

"There is much that is good in what Ewen said, but in some respects I agree with Bill Ruttle. There are two old maxims I have in mind. In this hundred and seventy-five year plan—"

"Five year plan," Ewen amended.

"We often hear of the start of a five year plan, do we ever hear of its end? It is generally followed by a second five year, then by another and so on. The first maxim is 'Union is Strength.' Most of us are where we are thanks to our Unions. We all dislike unofficial strikes, but if they spread they become official. To have a Grand Council that could squash them means withholding strike pay. Would not that cause anger and split the entire Socialist movement?"

"Sure it would," said Ruttle.

"My second maxim, and I almost hesitate to mention it seeing the princely hospitality we are enjoying, is 'Don't bite off more than you can chew.' I have never been more tempted to disregard it."

He pointed to the still laden table. There was a general laugh in which Lord Bethesda joined and the hard line of his lady's mouth relaxed into something of a smile.

"But I agree with Gwennie Wren if you unite too many people against you you accomplish nothing. You must proceed step by step. To try to take a flight of stairs in one leap means a crash with perhaps a bloody head and broke limbs. Without discussing Ewen's proposals in detail I think he wants to do too much too quickly. We all respect your lordship's judgment and experience, will you not tell us what you think about it?"

All eyes turned to their host. He did not rise but shook his head.

"Some of my son's views impressed me," he said. "Especially his ideal of a land without debt, but at this stage I express no opinion. It is for you younger men to get together and hammer out your programme. Then I might comment on it if asked to do so."

At this Joe Edmonds, Ewen's friend, spoke.

"We must think of it as a whole," he said. "Of course there are details to discuss but by and large it would make a new and better England."

Then Tom Dayton got up. He was the wild-looking man with long hair and an untidy beard who had been called Jeremiah. "I could go a long way with Ewen," he said, "but in his programme he omits the most important point of all—moral uplift. Our country is plunging headlong to ruin. Many of our popular papers are devoted mainly to sex and to the display of pictures of women as nearly nude as they dare. Modesty is a thing of the past and juvenile delinquency increases. There is talk of easier divorce and it was even suggested that a Bill should be brought in to legalise the very sin for which Sodom and Gomorrah were destroyed. Gambling is one of our greatest national industries. A few men are making huge fortunes out of the follies of the rest. The government shares the plunder. We spend far too much on drink and tobacco. I want to see sterner measures taken to stop these things. If this is not done our doom is certain. Who will have the courage to stop the rot?"

There was silence when he sat down. Then two or three others spoke, addressing themselves rather to what he had said than to Ewen's proposals. Some of them seemed frightened at what might seem an attack on the Unions and preferred to talk of other things.

"You will never stop gambling," Ted Boyne declared. "Why should you? To try to win a big prize is the hope that keeps many people going Nationalise the pools if you like but don't rob the average man of his dream of wealth and independence."

"Is that Socialism?" someone asked.

"We appreciate Dayton's ideals," Gibbons said, "but the taxes on tobacco and alcohol bring in about a thousand million a year to which the teetotal non-smoker contributes nothing. Can he suggest substitutes by which the moralist may pay a fair share?"

Others followed on somewhat similar lines. Then Lord Bethesda asked Major Bennion if he had anything to say.

"As a holder of Her Majesty's commission," Roger said, "I dissent entirely from your son's remarks as to the Monarchy. I am a Queen's man and always will be, together I think with all her loyal subjects. As to the other matters, I am no politician. Some of Ewen's proposals were possibly good, others seemed contradictory. He believes in the House of Commons and would have an Upper Chamber comprising the best brains in the country, but he also wants an omnipotent Grand Council of the Trade Unions. The country would therefore have two if not three governments! That would not work for long; it might mean Civil war. Then he talks of levying Death Duties while we are still alive! Does he appreciate the loss in annual income that would cause? You cannot cut a cow in half and expect the same flow of milk as before! For the rest, while we have a Royal Family that is tireless in good works and is an example to us all I agree with Miss Wren that the nation will not willingly lose them."

Roger had more applause than most of the speakers. Then Ewen sprang up, obviously disappointed at the reception of his proposals.

"I am sorry so many of you are not Socialists at all. I am, and I hope when we meet our friends on Sunday they will realise the need of an active Socialist programme. I would sooner work and wait for several elections than abandon my faith. I still hope when you think it over you will see that courage, not cowardice, should be our watchword."

7

In The Night The next word was from Lord Bethesda

"If you will excuse me, my wife and I will now withdraw. Drinks will be found in the lounge. This is Ewen's party and I hope he will see

40

you all get what you want. My niece will help. I do not know if you will be able to agree on your agenda but I trust you will all enjoy your stay here. I have to obey doctor's orders. So I wish you good night."

He went to Lady Bethesda and gave her his arm. Everyone stood up as they moved to the door.

"J.J. is very much my lord, isn't he?" Gibbons remarked when the couple had gone. J.J. stood for Jimmie Jones, and in the past Bethesda was often so known.

"Too wily to commit himself," Ruttle said, shrugging his broad shoulders.

If that were so, he was not the only one to doubt the wisdom of their proceedings. Ewen however acted on his father's suggestion. He led the way to the lounge where many varieties of drinks were waiting, from tea and coffee to whisky and old brandy. There were also tasty snacks of many kinds which were attacked as voraciously as if the company had not seen food for forty-eight hours. They broke into little groups and tongues wagged more freely. Ewen plied them with drinks, and the more they drank the more they agreed there was a lot in what he had said. They hoped the Party would support him. Each vowed he would if the others did.

Roger Bennion had a word here and there with different people and then met the acting host.

"Have you spoken yet with your father as to a new home?" he asked.

"No chance," Ewen said. "Y'know I'm beginning to be dam' sorry I brought you here."

"That is unfortunate. Why?"

"I never thought you would speak against me. Talk of milking half a cow! Things like that stick."

"I agreed with what you said as to the worker doing his best for the country," Roger replied. "You should not invite people unless you know their opinions. How many of these men will vote for you against the Party bosses?"

"Quite a number, I hope."

"Ruttle is not a keen supporter is he?"

"Jealousy really. In politics your enemies are not the fellows in the other Party but in your own. They want a job and are afraid you might get it. When I propose Ruttle for the Grand Council he will come in all right. That is why I asked him."

Then there was more brandy, more argument and more agreement. It continued for some time. Even Ruttle thought their differences could be adjusted. Everyone agreed that Ewen had a lot of good ideas.

"Let ush drink to the Ginger Group," someone said a little unsteadily. They did.

"And to Ginger Ewen," someone else proposed, pointing to his curly red hair.

This was honoured with laughter and cheers. Someone began to sing "For he's a jolly good fellow," but was hushed lest Lady Bethesda should be disturbed. So with just one more they decided to go to bed.

The ladies had retired some time before, and Roger had slipped away when they did. If the proceedings of the evening had been dull at the start, they were lively at the finish and before the night was through there was to be a touch of comedy—or farce.

The rooms that had previously given sanctuary to Brothers Gregory and Thomas were not large when the two became one, but there was no austerity. The bed was reasonably soft, hot and cold water were laid on and the furniture was adequate. Roger wondered who would have the apartments next to him and on the other side of the narrow corridor, bearing such names as Theodosius, Nathaniel and Zebedee.

He did not immediately go to bed. He donned his dressing-gown and slippers and started the letter he usually wrote to his wife Ruth when they were separated. There was plenty to tell her. He knew he would be interested in wan little Ambrose whose father was a lord. A lesson in how not to bring up a child. As to the political angle, he said he doubted if the Ginger Group would be a very large or united one. There was a touch of foreboding about his final paragraph.

"There appear to be many cross-currents and latent jealousies. I shall try to get away before their big meeting on Sunday. I have a feeling that some serious or even tragic clash might so easily occur. We will hope not!"

He added a few words of affection and then he heard voices outside his door. He opened it a little way and saw to his surprise that Sandra Henshaw and Gwennie Wren were there.

"Come in," Sandra was saying, and she and Gwennie disappeared in the space sacred to the memory of Brother Nathaniel.

Roger wondered what the two young women had in common.

Each apparently had been favoured by Ewen Jones, but that would hardly be a bond of friendship. The room was allotted to Sandra. Why should she invite the companionship of the woman who had been Ewen's mistress?

He heard other doors open and close. Then there was quiet. Apparently all were settled for the night. He had not heard Gwennie Wren leave but presumed she had done so. But a soft shuffling of approaching footsteps rekindled his curiosity. He looked out and saw Ewen himself; also in dressing-gown and slippers, seeking Nathaniel's shelter!

That was certainly odd. Roger had no wish to spy and he closed his door. Of what followed he heard little, but was later on to hear a good deal. Ewen opened the door very quietly but paused on the threshold when he saw the two young women together, for Gwen was still with Sandra. Both were fully clad, smoking cigarettes.

"Come in, Ewen," Gwen said. "What can we do for you?"

"I heard voices," he muttered awkwardly, rather thickly. "I thought it might be Rhoda. I have been looking for her, to ask her something about tomorrow." Then more resourcefully he added, "Whose room is this? I thought they were all shingle rooms."

"Rhoda is in the other wing," Sandra said.

"I must find her. But tell me how you thought things went tonight?"

"Were you satisfied?" she returned.

"More or lesh. A lot of 'em have neither guts nor brains. They follow the crowd. The great thing is to get a start." He slurred his words a little. He had perhaps over-estimated his brandy capacity.

"Is it a comfort to you to remember what someone said four hundred years ago?" Gwen asked sarcastically.

"Don't s'pose so. What was it?"

"Treason doth never prosper; what's the reason? Why, if it prosper, none dare call it treason."

"I am not concerned in treashon," he retorted angrily. "A dem-

democrashy can vote as it likes and if it votes for a change no sane person calls it treashon."

"Can one be false to one's friends, to one's Party and to one's Queen and not be guilty of treason?"

It must have been at about that point that Roger heard other footsteps approaching. This time there was no shuffling step. It was a firm tread that everyone might hear. Once again it stopped at the Nathaniel door. Roger could not resist the impulse to see who it was. At the me moment a voice from within—Sandra voice—told him.

"Ossie—what do you want?"

Captain Henshaw must have been as astonished as Ewen had been to find that his wife was not alone. He looked at the three of them and the words he had meant to say died on his lips. He was too surprised to close the door.

"Is this a committee meeting?" he muttered.

"In a way," Ewen replied. "I wondered what they thought of our dishcussion tonight."

"What do you want?" Sandra asked again. "I am getting sleepy." She stubbed out her cigarette.

"Have you—have you got my toothbrush?" he asked. "I cannot find it."

"How have you managed these last two days?" his wife asked derisively. "You packed your own bags. But of course the holy men here never used such things. Who knows when toothbrushes were invented?" She yawned.

"I agree with Sandra," Gwen said. "We had better all clear out and let her get to sleep."

"I might see if Rhoda has a spare one." This was Ewen's suggestion. The unexpected arrival of Sandra's husband had somewhat sobered him. He moved towards the door and the others followed. Then the door was locked and there was silence.

Roger was asking himself what it all meant. Why had Sandra wished to have Gwen with her? Why had Gwen stayed? What was the meaning of Ewen's stealthy arrival? Why had Oswald Henshaw followed him there?

44

Had he known what was to happen before another day was over he might have pondered the questions more deeply.

8

Morning and Afternoon

Many a poet has remarked that cool reflection comes with the morning. How far this applied to those who had finally applauded Ewen Jones overnight might be hard to say. When Roger went down to breakfast only three others were with him. Ewen and Rhoda as representing the host and hostess, and Jeremiah Dayton. The others were having the meal in their bedrooms. It was rumoured that the ladies did justice to the good things brought them; the men were mostly content with coffee and aspirin. Jeremiah being both an early-bedder and a teetotaller was his usual cheery self—if cheery be the right word.

"Were you able to provide Captain Henshaw with a spare toothbrush?" Roger asked Rhoda.

"Did he want one?" she replied.

"He decided he could manage," Ewen said.

He spoke rather shortly, wondering perhaps what Roger knew of the matter. It was the only reference to the odd happenings in the Nathaniel room.

"I do not want to suggest another world war in our time is inevitable," Jeremiah remarked, "but is it not an extraordinary thing that the end of the world as depicted in the Bible, fire from heaven, fugitives seeking refuge in caves, and mountains crashing on them is just what we imagine atomic warfare would be?"

He threw out the question as a sort of challenge, but no one seemed inclined to take it up. He persevered.

"According to prophecy the Armageddon that will start the final catastrophe is to be fought somewhere near the Garden of Eden where our history began, the Mesopotamia region more or less where our oil comes from. Is it fanciful to suppose that a fight for oil will start the conflict?"

He looked hopefully at the others, but no one was in the mood for such discussions. They ate in silence until Rhoda asked Roger what he would like to do that morning.

"I want to see Dan Floss." Roger said. "Shall I find him in his cottage?"

"If not, his wife will tell you where he is," she replied. Actually Dan was rolling the lawn when Roger found him. A bent figure of a man, he could not push the roller by hand. He had a sort of harness round his body and with slow steps was dragging it behind him. It was a pathetic sight, as in his younger days he had been very active and muscular. No doubt he wanted to show he was still of use, but to roll that vast lawn in such a way was beyond human possibility.

"I am Major Bennion. I believe you have applied for one of my father's cottages in London," Roger remarked after watching him for some moments.

"Aye, that be so," was the answer in broad country accent. "A cousin o' mine has one and I know some o' the folks there. A little bit house and a patch o' garden. I've allus wanted that."

He paused in his work and wiped his forehead. He was not a typical faithful old retainer. His voice was rough and his manner had a note of independence, blended perhaps with anger. He had worked hard all his life and felt it was unfair his poor gnarled hands should have let him down. The faithful retainer implies old and honoured employers. There may have been something lacking in that respect.

"Lord Bethesda wants your cottage for the new gardener?"

"Aye, leastwise 'er leddyship does."

"You know Mr. Ewen has one of our cottages?"

"Aye," was the laconic reply.

"What do you feel about that?"

"It doan seem fair. I doan say as I've any rights to it, but I've more rights nor he if what my cousin says be true."

"How long have you worked here?"

"Forty year. Long afore them come. I 'ad two three lads under me

46

then. Mostly I laid out the gardens as they is now. 'Er leddyship thinks one man with a motor mower and such like could keep it goin'. I can't manage motors." He held up his mis-shaped hands and added, "Me knees ain't much better."

"What help do you get now?"

"Two men from th' village 'casionally."

"That must leave you a lot to do."

"Aye. 'Er leddyship reckons I must give up."

"What has your cousin to say about it?" Roger asked.

"No use o' my repeatin' wot 'e said. If Sir Nick'las meant the places for the likes o' Mr. Ewen it bain't no business of ourn. I s'pose me and the missus'll get lodgin's somewhere. 'Er leddyship talks of an ejec'ment order."

Roger was inclined to like the old fellow. He was not obsequious, and his was the sort of case his father would like to help.

"I came down," he said, "to see if I could persuade Mr. Ewen to go. If he does you shall have the first offer of the place."

"That be mighty kind of 'ee sir. 'Twas what I allus 'oped for, something like that. I promise 'ee me and my missus'll keep it in good order and the bit of' garden we could manage fine."

"All right," Roger smiled: "My father may have to talk of ejectment orders, too."

He was carrying his rod and he strolled to the river to see if it looked hopeful for a cast. It was a bright morning and gave promise of a very hot day, not an angler's ideal by any means.

As he went along he saw Ambrose with a young woman, presumably his nursery governess. The little boy was clad as many other little boys were about that time in the outfit of a "Redskin." No doubt his colourful clothes and his bow and arrows were correct enough but how can anyone play Indians by himself? His rather stolid companion did not seem to enter into the spirit of the game at all.

"Hullo, Chief White Bull," Roger said "Out hunting?"

The boy looked solemnly at him and shook his head.

"You should, you know. Can you use the bow and arrows?"

"Her ladyship does not like him to kill things," the girl answered for him.

"Not much risk of that," Roger said. "Could you hit that tree?" Ambrose fitted an arrow to the bow. He made the shot and actually hit the tree. The arrow fell to the ground.

"Let me try," Roger said. His arrow, with more bend to the bow, penetrated the bark and stayed there. "Now you have another go."

He took the boy's hands and repeated the shot. The arrow struck close to the first. Little Ambrose was clearly delighted. "Again," he said.

They did it again and there were the three well-feathered arrows close together.

"I do not think her ladyship would like that," the girl said.

"Do you play with him sometimes?" Roger asked.

"I take him for his walks."

"But what is the use of dressing him up like this if he doesn't get any fun out of it?"

"I do as her ladyship wishes," was the prim reply. "We must go in now."

Roger gathered the arrows. It was not for him to interfere and she was obviously rather afraid of what had been done.

"Has he no playmates?" he asked.

"His little cousin comes sometimes."

"That is good. Farewell, brave-chief. We must have a real game someday."

Ambrose nodded and turned obediently towards the house. Roger strolled on past the hut to the stream.

He tried a few casts, but with no luck. He was thinking what a queer place he had come to. Some of Ewen's revolutionary ideas had surprised and shocked him. He recognised that many people who called themselves Socialists did not realise the logical consequences of their theories, but he could not conceive that the party as a whole would adopt his proposals. Lord Bethesda was no longer the roaring lion of the past. He was a sick man and it was doubtful if he would endorse his son's policy. It was certain Lady Bethesda would not and there was much to which orthodox Trade Unionists might well object.

Then he pondered over the curious gathering of the night before in

48

Sandra's room. What lay behind that? Did Sandra expect Ewen to visit her? If so, why had she pressed Gwennie Wren to stay? What was the meaning of the arrival of Ossie Henshaw? Was he suspicious?

That Sandra and Ewen were more than a little interested in one another was fairly obvious. She had lost her bet about the women's vote. Ewen had suggested payment in a special currency. Judging from her self-conscious expression that currency might be kisses. Or was it something more serious?

It was all rather baffling and he did not like to be baffled. Possibly Rhoda Rees might throw some light on things. She was intelligent as well as charming. And there was his own little plot to be remembered, the ejectment of Ewen after a word with his father. He was to get light on some of the matters before the day was through, though not from Rhoda.

When he went in for lunch he learned that many of the party had spent much of the morning exploring the neighbourhood. Lord Bethesda had chartered two motor coaches and invited those of his guests who cared to do so to visit some of the beauty spots of the neighbourhood. Nearly all of them had gone.

This not only put an edge on their appetites but gave them fresh topics for conversation. There was a good spread of cold viands and for the most part they helped themselves. Lady Bethesda did not appear. She was lunching in the nursery.

It was curious that no one seemed anxious to talk politics. If anyone started such themes there was generally a response "Let us see what they say tomorrow." The men had lost their headaches but many of them were not quite clear as to what they had committed themselves the night before. If, as we are told, wine is a mocker, what may not old brandy be?

"I met our young friend this morning," Roger remarked to Rhoda. "I was surprised at his warlike attire. Who is responsible for that?"

"It is rather a sad story," she replied. "Before Brigid came, that is about three months ago, he was in charge of a very nice girl, Myfanwy Lloyd."

"Also Welsh?"

"How clever of you," she smiled. "We do rather favour the Welsh. Myfanwy was teaching him to read and he was getting on quite well. But she also smuggled into the house some of those lurid illustrated papers about cowboys and Indians to read to him. He loved them. She always looked through them first to make sure they were not too blood-thirsty. She persuaded Aunt Connie to let him have that outfit. He looked sweet in it. But soon after that Aunt Connie unfortunately found some of the papers. She was furious and exit Myfanwy in a hurry. Aunt Connie would have destroyed the costume but I persuaded her not to. He might wear it sometimes when he was a very good boy. So that is how it happened."

"I am glad he has some boyish instincts," Roger said. "I taught him to shoot arrows. Don't let Brigid get thrown out for that!"

"I don't think she'll mention it. Nor will he. Aunt Connie dotes on him but he ought to have been a little girl."

"What does Brigid read to him?"

"Tales his mother chooses."

"Very improving, I expect. Do you ever read to him?"

"Never," Rhoda laughed. "I just tell him stories."

"That you make up?"

"No. There are some juicy bits in the Bible, you know. David and Goliath and Daniel in the lion's den."

Ewen was again sitting beside Sandra, but, although attentive to her wants, he seemed less buoyant than usual. It had become very hot and when someone suggested it would be pleasant to have a swim in the river later in the afternoon quite a number welcomed the idea.

"We will have tea on the lawn," Ewen said. "I will have the seats put out."

That also met general approval. Some of the non-swimmers may have mentally decided to go as far as those seats and no further.

When the meal was over Roger got a chance of a word with his host and decided to broach the real object of his visit. They were in a shady corner of a verandah and lit cigars, though Roger would have preferred his trusty briar.

"Were you aware of the nature of your son's proposals?" he asked as an opening.

"I was not," was Bethesda's short reply.

"If I may ask it, do you support them?"

50

It was some moments before there was a reply. Then—"All political movements need ginger at times, but dynamite is dangerous!"

Roger made no comment and after a further pause the old man went on—"I may have said some foolish things when I was young, but if you go too fast and too far you may find you are not leading a Party, you are leaving it. For progress the engine must pull the coaches, not rush on without them! But you are not interested in politics?"

"I am not an extremist in any direction," Roger said. "I like to understand things. But it was not politics that brought me here."

"What was it?"

Roger explained as briefly as he could his father's idea in creating his "folly" and the feeling that Ewen was not the sort of tenant for whom the cottages were intended.

"We had an application from your gardener Dan Floss for one of them. He has a cousin there. He seemed a suitable person but there was nothing vacant. That led to the discovery that your son had one, though it had not been let directly to him. I saw him and suggested he should go and Floss could have it. He said he could not afford to live elsewhere unless he was in some way assisted. He asked me to explain the matter to you. I do so with reluctance as it touches on things that are no concern whatever of mine. But that is how it stands."

Lord Bethesda looked very uncomfortable while Roger was speaking.

"Of course I knew his address," he said, "but I had no idea he was living in any way on the charity of your father or anyone else. He must go. As to his needing assistance, when I first went to the House there was no salary for the members. We had to manage as best we could with help from our local associations or a Trade Union. We got nothing like the salary he receives. I was married and had him to provide for. He lives alone, employing I believe a housekeeper. He should manage easily, unless he has expensive tastes. It has upset me very much. I will see him about it."

"Thank you," Roger said. He did not know if Gwennie Wren was an expensive taste, but it was not for him to mention her. "I did have a few words with Floss. May I tell him there is a prospect of his getting what he wants?"

"Leave it till I have seen Ewen," the father replied.

There was a pause. Then, abruptly changing the subject he said—"I believe I have heard of you, Major Bennion. Did you not have something to do with those murders at a golf club? Sir Cowdray Hood told me so."

"I tried to help."

"And before that there was what they called the Judas Kiss?"

"That is so."

"Are you still working with Scotland Yard?"

"Oh, no," Roger laughed. "Things just happened that way."

"You impressed Sir Cowdray very much."

"Nice of him to say so," Roger replied.

A little later he got his rod and made his way again to the river bank. He had spotted a wily old trout in the morning but had been unable to tempt it. As he crossed the lawn he saw several of the company in their shaded seats, already happily if not beautifully asleep. Open mouths are seldom becoming. A few had been in the water but most of them appeared content to bathe in the warm sunshine. They were suitably unclothed for the purpose. Both Sandra and Gwen had reduced their garments to a minimum. Very alluring, but he crept quietly by lest he should disturb anyone.

The spot he was seeking was a little down-stream in the shade of a dangling willow. He soon got busy. He had a fly he called Devil's Charm, gaudy and fairly large. He did not expect it to be successful but he thought it might attract attention if the fish were still there. It was, but although he made three casts there was nothing doing.

He changed it for Baby's Breath, a dainty and fluffy thing which he laid carefully just where the contemptuous old trout lurked. He withdrew it almost as quickly. After another cast or two he changed it for the Angel's Kiss. This he drew more slowly and his victim became alert. It seemed to be thinking it foolish to miss so much good food. Perhaps its appetite grew keener. Another tempting cast—a rush—and a good bite. The old trout sped away and the fight was on.

It was only a matter of time. Roger had plenty of patience and knew his job. In due course the speckled monster—not perhaps quite as large as he had thought, but a good two-pounder—lay on the bank.

He tried again but with no further luck. He glanced at his watch and

52

saw it was later than he had supposed. The bathers would have gone back for tea. Putting his rod and his flies away—the Angel's Kiss in his cap as a mark of triumph—he walked to the broad path that led to the lawn.

As he approached the hut he heard a voice.

"Major Bennion!"

It came from the hut. He turned towards it and the voice came again. Sandra's voice.

"That beast Gwennie Wren took part of my costume to mend it. Can you get me a coat or something?"

"Will my jacket do?"

"Do you mind?"

"Not in the least. I will shut my eyes!"

A white arm came through the narrowly opened door and took the coat. A few moments, later Sandra emerged clad in his jacket with the briefest of briefs beneath it.

"What happened?" he asked.

"The others left us. Then Gwen said the string of my bra was broken—or she broke it. She said she would run in and mend it or would bring me a coat. I was to wait in the hut. We hadn't a spare stitch between us. It must have been at least half an hour ago. She did it purposely. There is no way to the house except across the lawn where they are having tea. She wanted me to look a fool before them all!"

Sandra spoke in short, angry sentences. If what she said was true it was certainly a nasty trick for one girl to play on another. Roger had often wondered how the female of the species could approach so closely to nudity and yet place such importance on the remaining strips of ribbon. Sandra was a finely developed young woman and it would undoubtedly have caused some sensation if she had approached the party as a human mermaid!

"I thought you and Gwen were such friends," he said.

"What made you think that?"

"Your room is just across the passage from mine. Last night I heard you ask her in."

"She did not need much asking! Did you hear anything else?"

"I thought Ewen and your husband joined you."

She laughed bitterly. "Quite a party, wasn't it? She hates me."

They were then in full sight of the company on the lawn. Gwen was sitting in a low chair with a wrap over her shoulders. She was making a good and leisurely meal.

"Oh, Sandra," she cried. "Sorry I was so long. I couldn't find any thread and I just had to have a cup of tea."

"What happened?" Ewen asked. "I was just coming to look for you."

Sandra did not reply. She strode on to the house. Roger took attention from her by displaying his catch.

"Some people have all the luck," Gwen said to him with a mischievous smile.

9

Tragic Night

Dinner that evening was a more sociable affair than it had been the night before. For one thing the guests, particularly the womenfolk had become better acquainted and so were more chatty. For another, there were no speeches. Politics were left alone. A further reason may have been that Lady Bethesda told them there was a play on television that her husband wished to see and which he thought might interest them. It lasted about an hour and they could resume their discussions afterwards if they desired to do so. It started at 8.15 so the meal was a little shorter than previously.

They mostly occupied the same seats as before. Sandra was again next to Ewen and as Gwennie Wren was on the same side of the table they could not exchange the hostile glances they might have done had they been vis-à-vis.

Roger was pleased to find himself still beside Rhoda. She was looking very pretty, and said in answer to his question that she had not seen her Jeremy that day.

"A martyr to duty," he smiled.

"No worse than having a class of children to look after," she said.

"Meaning us? You were in charge of the tea?"

"More or less."

"Did our Gwennie make a good meal?"

"I think so. Did you miss her?" Her green eyes sparkled at him.

"I did not, but someone did."

In a low tone he told of his rescue of the forlorn Sandra. "Did Gwennie go to the house for a needle and thread?"

"Not as far as I know. Had she asked me or one of the maids she could have had them at once."

"So I imagined. What would you have done in Sandra's place?"

"It couldn't happen to me. If I sunbathe I do not walk about quite so airily and I always have a wrap. But it was a mean trick, especially with all these fat old men about."

"That is begging the question. Had you been Sandra what would you have done?"

"Probably have waited for help as she did. Or I might have fashioned an apron of leaves like Eve."

"A good idea, if adequate," he smiled. "Has Gwen been here often?"

"Two or three times with Ewen for week-ends. I rather thought he to marry her."

"He is a man of errant tastes?"

"He is impetuous," Rhoda said. "I am fond of him, but he may get into trouble if he is not careful."

"With the Henshaws? What about them?"

"They have been here before. I like Sandra, but I hope Ewen won't be silly about her."

"Enough of them," Roger said. "Tell me more about Jeremy. Is he impetuous?"

"Not in the same way. He is very determined."

They chatted on and with that and some attention to the lady on his other side the time passed. It was on the whole a quiet meal. The host and hostess had little to say, while the male guests were mostly men of one-track minds. Some of them no doubt had amusing stories to tell in a smoking room, but that did not seem the occasion for them. Their women could generally discuss the Royal Family at considerable length and the prices of fish and vegetables, but such themes also appeared out of place. The food and wines again were good; they received due attention.

"Are you seeing the television?" Roger asked Rhoda.

"I don't know. It is a story founded on the Battle of Britain. A lot of shooting and that sort of thing. We have had it before. I do not really care for it, though uncle does."

"Not in my line either," Roger said. "I had my share of the real thing. I think I will give it a miss."

Most of the others however, decided to see it and went with their host and hostess to the room specially fitted for its reception.

Roger went to the billiards room where Captain Henshaw promptly challenged him to a game of snooker. Old "Jeremiah" Dayton followed them as an onlooker, but he found a comfortable chair and was soon asleep. It was a very warm night. There seemed thunder in the air.

"What will you play for?" Ossie asked. "A tenner?"

"I am not a robber," Roger laughed, "and I don't want to be robbed. A quid if you like."

"Twenty shillings? I thought you would say twenty pounds."

"I play for the fun of the game. A pound is my limit."

Reluctantly Ossie agreed. He was expert with the cue and the balls ran his way. He won fairly easily.

"I was lucky," he said. "What start do you want to play for a tenner?"

"No start," Roger replied. "Level terms again for another quid."

He did not mean to be lured as his trout had been that afternoon! But he was by no means a poor player and that time things went kindly. He had two good breaks and a fine run at the end, winning by a narrow margin.

"Major Bennion, if you have finished, there is something I want to ask you." This was from "Jeremiah" who had woken from his little nap.

"Certainly," Roger said. "You do not want to play any more, Henshaw?"

"No. I think I'll get a little fresh air. Very hot in here." He walked out. Why waste time playing for doubtful shillings?

Roger took a seat opposite the old man and lit his pipe. "You are not a TV fan?" he asked.

"Certainly I am not. Our only hope for sanity is to avoid it. That and the radio pour out a turgid stream of so-called instruction and amusement all day and far into the night. Religion followed by jazz. Science and low comedy, dancing and sport, politics and buffoonery. They pump poison into us. There is no time for reading or for thought. What sort of people shall we become?"

"We still have the right to switch off," Roger said. "One of the few privileges left us. What was it you wished to ask me?"

"What we were talking about last night. Is it an indictable offence for Members of Parliament to discuss deposing the Monarch to whom they have sworn fealty."

"Perhaps it ought to be." Roger said, "But we pride ourselves on freedom of speech. Some people have always had Republican ideas."

"Should they enter parliament and take that oath without abandoning them? You would not?"

"Certainly not," Roger smiled, "but I have no parliamentary ambitions. Britain has been at its greatest under its Queens: Elizabeth, Anne and Victoria. Things are not too bright at the moment but, as Ewen said, Elizabeth the Second may be the greatest of them all."

"I would like to think so." "Jeremiah" nodded, rubbing a hand through his whiskers. "I did not hear it all very clearly. I was thinking more of the end of things. Is that at hand? The signs all point that way. Can you believe that man will know how to destroy the World without someone wanting to try?"

"Yes, if the man would thereby destroy himself."

"But if a Hitler, making a bid for world power, knew he had failed, would he not destroy himself and humanity, if he had the means of doing so, rather than give in?"

"Possibly," Roger said, not wishing to prolong the discussion. "But talking of Queens, I have sometimes wondered if we should do better if the royal descent was in the female line. There have been many notable Queens in history; Catherine the Great of Russia, Maria Theresa, Cleopatra, Balkis the Queen of Sheba, Boadicea, Theodora—"

"Who was Theodora? I haven't heard of her."

"Some woman in her day," Roger said. "Early sixth century I believe. A slave, a circus performer, a courtesan and finally an empress. She married Justinian and they ruled the Roman Empire on a fifty-fifty basis. She was the better man of the two. When there was a rebellion the Emperor would have run away but she told him the best shroud was the imperial purple. They won through. Bees and ants have queens, so have wasps. In some ways it is easier and more chivalrous for men to serve under a Queen—"

He was speaking half in jest, but there was a sudden crash of thunder that seemed to shake the house. He went to the window and pulled back the curtain. "A real storm at last," he said. "It should clear the air a bit." Further peals followed, with vivid flashes of lightning. But "Jeremiah" disregarded them.

"I am not really a party man," he rambled on. "People think I am a pessimist, but I am not—unless a pessimist is a disappointed idealist. If there is no spiritual awakening Britain's doom is certain. Eat, drink and be merry seems to be our motto. Do you believe in an afterlife, Major Bennion?"

It was a strange change of subject. Stranger still had they known what was happening at that moment.

"I once put that question to an eminent archaeologist and geologist," Roger replied. "Had his researches into the remote past, before man appeared on earth, given him any idea as to his future?"

"And his answer?"

"He said definitely yes. The more we understood the past the better we realized its plan and its ordered progress until its object, Man, was attained. It was impossible to believe that the Creator, or the Originator, would thereupon scrap His wonderful achievement. There must be further progress, though what form it would take he could not tell, any more than the first jelly fish could foresee homo sapiens!"

"He was right," "Jeremiah" said. "It would be senseless—"

Suddenly he stopped: There was a scream, a piercing scream, very different from the thunder.

"What was that?" Roger cried. "It came from the TV room. I must see."

Captain Henshaw had left the door open. The hall was in darkness but light showed through the obscured glass panel in the adjacent door of the television room. As Roger opened it a swirl of wind blew forward the heavy window curtains, almost threatening to upset the apparatus that stood in front of them. Hastily he closed the door.

It was a curious sight that he beheld. A ceiling light was on; the TV set was not functioning. Most of the people were standing. They clustered round something he could not at first see, in the front row of the seats. Some of them looked at him when he entered. Pale, with horror in her eyes, Rhoda came to him.

"It is Ewen," whispered. "He—he is dead!"

"Struck by lightning?"

"I—I don't think so."

Lord and Lady Bethesda were standing beside the recumbent figure on the central seat just in front of the TV set. The others surrounded them. Shock and horror showed in every face.

Roger went forward. They made way for him. But for the fact that his head was sunk on to his chest Ewen might still have been looking at the picture. Blood was trickling down his cheek and more blood was staining his soft white shirt. He was leaning back in his chair, his hands hanging inertly at the sides. Roger took one of them. There was little doubt the man was dead. He examined the TV set. Was it possible that some mechanism there could have caused so terrible an accident? He could hardly believe it, even in such a storm. The light came on at once and soon a voice was speaking normally, though with crackles due to atmospheric disturbance. He switched off. Another flash of lightning and a roll of thunder followed by shrill screams from some of the women added further grimness to the scene.

"What happened?" Roger asked.

"He has been shot," Lord Bethesda replied in a hoarse tone. "You understand these things. What must we do?" He was obviously suffering from the shock and seemed quite unable to deal with the tragic situation.

59

At his word Roger took command. He felt the horror of the occasion but he knew what had to be done.

"Rhoda," he said, "will you please telephone your uncle's doctor. Tell him what has happened and ask him to inform the police and request them to come at once."

Then he turned to the rest of the company.

"Will you all return to the seats you were occupying while you were watching the picture."

"The police!" some of them muttered.

"What do our seats matter if he was shot from outside?" Lady Bethesda asked. "He must have been. The window was open." She was pale and spoke with some effort.

"That we have to be sure of," Roger replied. "Please do as I say."

No one questioned it and, as they moved, the body moved, too. It remained in the chair but rolled a little to one side. They were deep arm-chairs, no doubt very comfortable. Roger raised the sagging head. It appeared there were two wounds, one in the right eye and the other lower down in the region of the heart. Either might have been speedily fatal.

"Did anyone leave the room?"

No one answered, except that one woman muttered it was dark.

"If there were shots, did anyone hear them?"

Again there was no reply though Mrs. Doodell said there was shooting and bombing all the time and after that the thunder.

Roger glanced round the room. The TV apparatus stood in the recess of the bay window. It was a fairly large box showing a seventeen-inch picture. It stood on four stout legs high enough to give good vision for all: In front of it were five rows of seats, each with five chairs except the one nearest the screen where there were only three. No doubt the picture would be distorted from the extreme side. Fourteen seats were now occupied leaving nine empty.

On the centre of the three front seats, the dead man sprawled. No one claimed the seat on either side of him.

"Did he sit there alone?" Roger asked.

"He liked to be able to turn the knobs," Lady Bethesda said. "Most people prefer to be further back."

She was sitting with her husband in the last row of all, at the side. Then Rhoda returned.

"They are coming," she said in a very subdued voice.

"Where did you sit?" Roger asked her.

"I thought it was here." She indicated the first seat in the third tow.

"I sat here," said Mrs. Boyne who was already in occupation. "Next my husband."

"I was a little late and it was dark," Rhoda admitted. "It was an end seat; I thought it was that."

"You are right," Sandra said from the seat behind. "You touched my shoulder when you came in. I think that lady and gentleman had moved up to be nearer the centre."

"That's right, Lil," Mr. Boyne said. "I was straight behind Ewen. Might have been shot myself!"

That left eight vacant chairs.

"It was light enough for you to recognise her?" Roger asked Sandra.

"I wouldn't say that, but I knew who it was. Later, of course, when the light came on, I saw her."

"Was it dark in the hall when you came in?" Roger enquired, this time of Rhoda.

"There was a light in the front part. It was dark here."

"Is that usual?"

The girl hesitated. "Uncle Jim likes it dark. If people come in and go out it is rather an interruption when the light outside is on."

Roger noted the switch by the door. It apparently turned on the ceiling light that illumined the whole room. There are more modern appliances that throw the light upwards and so leave a soft glow in the that does not affect the picture. Since visitors were infrequent and the Bethesdas were generally alone they had not troubled about that.

"No one heard the shots," Roger remarked. "When was the tragedy discovered?"

"When the lights went on," Mrs. Boyne said.

"Who turned them on?"

"I did," Lady Bethesda replied. "The picture ended. There was silence except for the thunder. Then something started we didn't want to see. So I switched on the light and called to Ewen to turn off. Then someone screamed. I think it was Mrs. Doodell or Miss Wren."

"It wasn't me," Gwen said.

"I couldn't help it," Mrs. Doodell muttered. "He hadn't moved so I bent forward to speak to him.... It was horrible."

"I screamed, too," Mrs. Dayton said. "His head was sunk forward and I saw the blood."

"A great shock," Roger said sympathetically. "The picture was showing, I believe, from 8.15 to 9.15. The thunderstorm started as far as I can judge just after nine."

"There were atmospherics before that," Joe Edmonds remarked.

"Yes, but if the shots came from outside they would probably have been before the storm."

"Why so?" one of the men asked.

"Anyone would have been soaked in a few minutes and might have been shown up by the lightning. Did any of you speak to Ewen or notice him in any way during the play?"

Sandra answered. "Someone asked for it to be louder. But that was near the beginning. I think it was Lady Bethesda."

"That is right," the lady said. "His lordship is slightly deaf: We could hear the noises but not the words. Ewen was all right then."

"I have made a rough sketch showing where you were all sitting. Is it correct?"

Roger passed it to Lord Bethesda who took it with rather a shaky hand.

"I think so—except—"

"Naturally we do not know where everyone sat," Rhoda remarked. "A few moved, like Mr. and Mrs. Boyne, and one or two came in later."

"How late? When the play had started or later than that?"

"Soon, after it started."

"Can any of you recall anyone else who was here for any part of the time and is not here now?"

There was no reply. They mostly shook their heads. "And no one left?"

Again there was no answer, except that Lady Bethesda said, "They could hardly do that without obstructing our view."

Then the door opened. Dr. Strange and the police had arrived.

10

Among Those Missing

Once again the window curtains billowed and the door was quickly shut. The storm had lessened but not fully abated.

Dr. Strange, an elderly man with greying hair, was accompanied by Inspector Bellairs of the local police and two constables. At a sign from Roger the doctor and the inspector went forward to look at Ewen's body. They were soon satisfied that life was extinct. The doctor, of course, recognised him and glanced round the room. He saw his old patient at the back and went across to him.

"This is very very distressing," he said. "You and Lady Bethesda have my deepest sympathy. How are you feeling yourself?"

"Not very well," Lord Bethesda replied shakily. "I would like to go to my room if I may. Major Bennion can tell you all about it."

"Everyone might go," Roger said "We are all staying in the house. Here is a chart showing where each one is sitting now, and where, as far as they know, they were sitting when the shots were fired. There are five other guests who were not present. I did not come in until afterwards."

The inspector took the chart and checked it with the numbers in each row.

"The windows open inwards," Roger added. "They and the curtain meet just behind the television set. The room is said to have been in darkness and it would seem possible for the shots to have been fired from outside, between the supports of the cabinet."

"Good shooting in the dark—if this man was the intended victim," Inspector Bellairs remarked.

"Good shooting up to a point," Roger agreed. "The light of the picture would to some extent show up the face and the white shirt of the person just in front of it, to anyone outside. A range of only a few feet. I have not touched the window—left it for you to examine."

"Quite so," said Bellairs. "I brought along the photographer. He shall take a flash or two of everyone as they are sitting; then they can go. I may want to see them later and, of course, no one must leave the house."

"Other guests are due tomorrow," Roger said. "I take it, Lord Bethesda, you will not wish them to come?"

"No. Indeed no," was the reply.

"I will arrange that with Rhoda. I expect she has their names and addresses or telephone numbers."

Rhoda nodded. She was an efficient secretary and saw how the arrival of thirty more visitors would add vastly to the confusion. A good thing Roger had thought of it so soon. The cameraman did his job, then Lord and Lady Bethesda, followed by the others, left the room.

"I will see you presently," the doctor said to his lordship. "Get him to bed," he added to his wife. "He may need a sedative. It is a very very shocking business."

Lady Bethesda nodded. "I liked the idea of this meeting but no one would imagine such a terrible thing could happen here."

"I would like to see the ladies' handbags as they go out," Bellairs said, "and my assistant will feel the men's pockets—just as a matter of routine."

No one protested and it was soon done. Roger had a word with Rhoda, the last to leave. He asked her to telephone the guests whose numbers she had and to say that owing to a fatal accident to Ewen the meeting for Sunday was cancelled. To the others she could send telegrams to be delivered first thing in the morning. "'Owing to Ewen's sudden death meeting cancelled.' Sign it Bethesda."

"Was it an accident?" she enquired.

"I am afraid not. If you are pressed with questions just say the police have the matter in hand; you do not know any more. No doubt particulars will appear in the Press."

Dr. Strange had made a cursory examination. "We know the approximate time of death," he said. "You must arrange for the ambulance to remove the body. I will extract the bullets and let you have them. There is nothing further I can do here. I will see his lordship."

"The direction of the bullets may be important," Roger said.

"Yes, yes. I will see to that."

The doctor was visibly upset. When he had gone the inspector surveyed every chair and every corner of the room. He found no weapon and nothing that seemed likely to help him. He pulled back the curtains and looked at the windows. Rain was still falling but the storm had passed.

"As you said, Major Bennion, anyone standing outside would only have to open the window a few inches and part the curtains to get a clear shot. Too dark I suppose for anyone inside to see anything?"

"It was very dark and very still before the storm," Roger replied.

"There is no question of some sort of infernal machine in the set itself?"

"I should say none. Apparently it was functioning all the time and it still does. I tried it. Of course it can be examined, but any sort of explosion would have put it out of action and every body would have seen it."

"We will examine it," Bellairs said, "but I do not doubt you are right. I will have a look into the room from the outside, with the light on and off."

"Do it carefully. There is a narrow flower-bed in front of the window. The heavy rain will probably have obliterated foot-marks on it and on the path. I should be inclined to put a man on guard and leave it until daylight. You could try the casements for finger-prints, though if there are any they may show better when dry."

"That is true," Bellairs said. "I will shine a light on the window from a little way off to get a general impression."

"It is for you to say," Roger replied.

He followed him across the hall to the front door. As they reached it Captain Henshaw walked in. He was bareheaded and his clothes were very wet.

"Been having a walk in the rain?" Roger asked him.

"More of a run," Ossie said. "I've never been in such a storm."

"Why did you go out?" Bellairs enquired.

"To get some air," was the haughty reply.

"There has been trouble. Mr. Ewen Jones was shot, apparently from outside. I am a police inspector. If you will come in I would like to ask you a few questions."

"Ewen shot? Is that true, Bennion? Is he hurt?" Oswald Henshaw sounded startled and incredulous.

"It is quite true," Roger said gravely. "The shots were fatal."

"My God! Poor devil!" Henshaw muttered. "Did he shoot himself?"

'There is no gun," Bellairs said. "What can you tell us?"

"Me? Nothing at all. I was not here."

They returned to the TV room. Bellairs produced his note and took Ossie's name and address. "You were here as one of Lord Bethesda's guests?"

"Yes. Asked by Ewen, who is an old friend."

"It was a big party. Was it a special occasion?"

"Major Bennion can tell you as much about that as I can. It was really a political pow-wow. Mostly M.P.s and their wives."

"Are you an M.P.?"

"Good Lord, no!"

"Then why were you here?"

Henshaw hesitated. "You are not an M.P., Bennion," he said. "Why are you here?"

"I came to see Lord Bethesda on a matter of business," Roger replied.

"Why are you here?" the inspector repeated.

"My wife and I were here days ago. Ewen was to outline a new political programme. Politics are not my line but I

66

suppose I am a more or less intelligent voter. He was trying it on the dog."

"You did not come to this room with the others?"

"Neither did Major Bennion. He and I had a game of billiards. Then, as it was so hot, I went out to get a breath of air."

"Before the storm?" Roger asked.

"Yes. I crossed the lawn and thought it might be cooler by the river. Suddenly the storm broke. I have never seen anything like it. Thunder, lightning and rain. Hell let loose. There is a hut near the river. I was more than half-way there, so I made a bolt for it. And then I was stuck until the rain stopped. That is all I can tell you. I was pretty well soaked and I wished I had made for the house instead."

"Did you see or meet anyone?" Roger enquired.

Ossie considered. "As a matter of fact I did see someone. Near the house, when I started out. I didn't see him clearly, he was some way off. I thought he was one of the men about the place, a gardener or something."

"Have you a pistol or firearm of any sort, Captain Henshaw?" the inspector asked.

"Good Lord, no! At least I have, but not here. If you can think up any more questions wait till I have changed my clothes and had a drink. I don't want pneumonia!"

With that he got up and left them. Bellairs did not attempt to detain him.

"What do you think of that, Major Bennion? Do you know him well?"

"Very slightly. I have met him and his wife two or three times. What he said about the billiards is true. We had two games and then he went out."

"More or less at the time the shooting was done?"

"Possibly, though that might have been at any time from 8.20 until the storm started."

"Why before it started?"

"I doubt if anyone would have gone out while it was on. They would have been soaked."

"As Henshaw was," Bellairs said, "and the thunder would mask the shooting. I wonder what man he saw—if there was one. I did not care for his manner. Who were the other members of the party who were not seeing the TV?"

"Tom Dayton, an M.P. He remained with me when Henshaw went out. We were discussing various things until we heard the screams when Ewen was found dead. So that clears him. There were two other M.P.s. Bill Ruttle and Fred Gibbons. I have no idea what they were doing. You might ask them."

"I will. You mean unless it was Henshaw it must have been one of them?"

"I would not be so definite as that. If the shot was from outside it opens wide possibilities."

"Enemies from anywhere?"

"Yes—if they knew about the TV show and where Ewen would be sitting."

"It is an inside job all right," Bellairs said, looking again at the chart. "You asked the doctor as to the direction of the shots. What was in your mind? Could anyone in the room have done it?"

"Not easily."

"But it was dark and everyone's attention was on the picture. There was room for anyone in the side seats to creep along the wall to the curtain and get near enough to fire the shots."

Roger did not immediately reply. He also studied his chart. "This would apparently give us Miss Gwennie Wren at seat 9," the inspector went on, "and on the other side Rhoda Rees in seat 13 and Sandra Henshaw in seat 18. Also possibly Mrs. Doodell in 5 and Mrs. Dayton in 7 as the seats between them and the wall were empty."

"All women."

"Women nowadays can be handy with a gun," Bellairs said, pleased with his idea.

"I considered all that," Roger answered, "but I do not think it possible. Much too risky. The person who fired the shots could not be certain the victim would not fall over or cry out. The lights might have come on and the killer would have been revealed, pistol in

68

hand. No. I am convinced the shots were from outside. By direction I was thinking rather of elevation."

"Then that leaves us with Henshaw and the two M.P.s you mentioned. Also of course the man Henshaw saw and Mr. Unknown who happened upon the scene and found everything ready for him."

The last remark was a little sarcastic. Roger for a moment studied Inspector Bellairs. He was a young man, confident of his powers and anxious no doubt to show his ability.

"If you take my advice," Roger said, "you will get hold of your Chief as quickly as you can, telling him how things stand and suggesting he asks Scotland Yard to come along at once. Please do not think I doubt your capacity but consider the sensation this is going to cause. Here, in Lord Bethesda's home, his son, a Member of Parliament, is shot. There are six or seven other Members in the house, too, and a lot more were due to morrow, though I hope I have stopped them."

"We do not call in the Yard until we find we cannot deal with a job ourselves," the inspector said, a little haughtily.

"This is no ordinary job—if murders are ever ordinary. Another thirty or so Members are being told what has happened. They will hurry to the House on Monday to ask questions. One of the first will be what are the Yard doing about it? I pity all you local people if it has to be said the Yard was not informed."

"There is that," Bellairs admitted, reluctant to lose the chance of a lifetime.

"See Ruttle and Gibbons by all means, but they can wait. Use my name if you like. The Assistant Commissioner knows me and not long ago he asked me to help Superintendent Yeo in the Greenham Golf Club mystery. You can say I think it urgent."

Roger was emphatic, and he had the satisfaction of seeing his advice acted on. Bellairs went to the telephone and returned a few minutes later to say the Chief Constable for the district had been contacted. He was taking the necessary steps and meanwhile the local questioning was to continue. Bellairs was a little more deferential in his manner. The Chief Constable knew of Roger Bennion and if the big man at the Yard knew him, too, it made a difference.

Bill Ruttle, big and breezy, came into the room when summoned.

69

"This is a nasty business," he said. "I have just been told about it. I suppose there can be no mistake? Who did it?"

"I am hoping you can help us," the inspector replied. "You did not see the television play?"

"I did not. Waste of time."

"Where were you? What were you doing? How did you spend your evening?"

"I was in my bedroom reading. I had brought a detective story with me and was rather anxious to see how it ended."

"You can let me see the book?"

"Certainly," Gibbons smiled. "I will give it you, if you like. It is by a good author but rather below standard. Too many characters and none very interesting. There is dope-traffic. A serious thing of course, but already used too often. That at least is my opinion; you may think otherwise."

"I am not concerned with story books but in the death of Ewen Jones," the inspector said sharply. Gibbons was too loquacious. "Did you leave the house during the evening?"

"My dear inspector, I thought I had answered that. I was in my room reading."

"You did not go out at all? Your shoes are wet."

Gibbons pushed forward his patent leather shoes of which the patent had long expired.

"They are rather," he smiled a little ruefully. "I am afraid I am somewhat careless about such things. At home a woman looks after them for me. Last night I did go a little way and I think I trod in a flower-bed. Tonight I just went into the porch. I wanted to find a four for bridge but everyone seemed keen on the TV play except two or three who made for the billiards room. So I went to my room to finish my book. I came down when I had done so and met everyone pouring out of the TV room. They told me what had happened. Poor old Ewen. I wish I could help you, inspector. I can only urge you to leave no stone unturned to catch the villain guilty of so foul a crime."

"We never do," Bellairs replied. "Nor do we leave any avenue unexplored." The smug clichés always annoyed him. "Have you a gun, Mr. Gibbons?"

"Gracious, no! I only fired one once in my life. That was in a country fair, at a bottle. Only three or four yards away and I missed it."

"Never in the Army?"

"No. My eyes. And I was already in the House. My duty lay there. I did my best for our boys."

At that Bellairs let him go.

"A real gas-bag, Major Bennion. What do you think of him? What about his dirty shoes?"

"The mud was dry. That might let him out. Had he been up to mischief tonight. I think he would have cleaned or changed them. There was one, morsel of sense in all he said."

"Glad to hear it. What was it?"

"You may have to consider Ewen's private life as well as the political opinions he expressed. That is where the Yard comes in."

11

While Others Slept

Inspector Bellairs departed to report more fully to his superintendent. He left two constables in charge, one inside and one outside the premises, with instructions that no one was to leave. He had had a word with the domestic staff and learned they were favoured with a wireless set of their own which was in full blast while they attended to the washing up and other domestic chores. Each answered for the rest.

It was some time before the guests separated and went to bed. They clustered in small groups and tried to find an explanation for the tragedy. Apparently with no success, though the general opinion was that the shooting must have been from outside and that some enemy from the village was probably responsible for it.

They plied Major Bennion with questions, but he said he could tell them nothing they did not already know. He would have liked to go to his room but waited to see if he could help Rhoda. She, poor girl, was hardest hit of all of them. She was fond of her cousin Ewen. She had sent her messages but felt it up to her to see everyone settled for the night before she herself retired. With Ewen gone and with her uncle and aunt upstairs everything devolved on her.

"Sleep as well as you can, my dear," Roger told her finally. "Everything will be in good hands tomorrow."

He then went to his own room and all was quiet. He did not write to Ruth. He knew she would be worried at his being concerned in another murder mystery but he might be able to tell her more about it before anything appeared in any paper she was likely to see. He did not anticipate there would be any of the odd visits of the night before. He lit a pipe and sat down to think things over.

Of the three suspects, as Inspector Bellairs regarded them, Henshaw, Ruttle and Gibbons, the first seemed to him the most likely. None of them had a clear alibi, but Ossie Henshaw not have failed to notice the marked attentions Ewen had been paying to his wife Sandra.

He, like the others, had called Ewen his friend, but why, unless he distrusted him, had he followed him to his wife's room the night before? The toothbrush excuse was such a feeble one.

Ossie had not been anxious for a third game of billiards. He had gone out and if the window of the TV room was slightly open because it was such a warm night, he might have listened for a few moments to the play. He could well have parted the curtains to peep inside. He would then have looked straight at the face of the man he distrusted, faintly visible in the light of the screen. He would hardly have been carrying his weapon but, if he had brought it with him, it would be a matter of moments to fetch—and use—it.

Then he must get rid of it. The river. That would explain the dash across the lawn and his getting caught in the storm. A more reasonable explanation than his story of a rush to the hut for shelter. Would he not have returned to the house directly the rain started? Who could say how long the storm would last?

It was a theory he, Roger, had not mentioned to Bellairs but it seemed more reasonable than to suspect the two M.P.s, who were accustomed to show their differences and had other ways of dealing with them.

Apart from Ossie it was rather a mixed bag of M.P.s that Ewen had gathered to hear what was to prove his last oration. All, no doubt, big men in their own constituencies, but only four of them stood out as definite personalities. Foremost was Bill Ruttle, a grim Socialist of the older order He had worked in the mines as a boy in the bad old days. The iron of privation had bitten into his soul and the capitalist would always remain an enemy from whom only evil could come.

Fred Gibbons, years younger, was of the doctrinaire type. He had been to a school of economics and had adopted politics as a profession. A fluent speaker, he knew how to make his audience laugh. That always was a help.

"Jeremiah" Dayton was of yet another type. A relic of a bygone age. In his youth he had possessed a fine voice and had once won a bardic prize at an Eisteddfod. He was earnest and sincere and his fellow Welshmen no doubt loved him, even if some of them thought him a bit crazy.

As for Joe Edmonds, he was less colourful but stood out as Ewen's best friend.

At this point Roger was disturbed by a knock on his door. He opened it. Outside stood Gwennie Wren in her night attire and a dressing-gown.

"I saw your light was on," she whispered. "I must have a word with you."

She slipped past him into the room.

"Will it not wait until the morning?" he asked.

"No, no! It is urgent. Never mind the proprieties. Do you know who shot Ewen?"

She seemed unusually agitated. He could almost see her breasts rising and falling as she spoke. He decided he must hear what she had to say but it was best to take the matter coolly.

"I do not," he said. "Sit down."

She took the chair and he sat on the edge of the bed. She had evidently come in some haste. Her pyjamas were of a flimsy, semi-transparent material and she was holding her wrap together with one hand. Her hair was untidy and she was in no way glamourised. That perhaps was reassuring!

"Do you believe I did it?" she asked just audibly.

"The inspector considered the possibility, as you were in an end seat," he replied. "I thought it unlikely."

"Thank God for that! I have just found this among my clothes!"

She put her hand in the dressing-gown pocket and pulled out a small but very ugly snub-nosed revolver.

"Don't point it at me," he said. "Your finger is on the trigger. Put it on the bed."

She did so.

"Yours?" he asked.

"No!"

"Ever had one?"

"Never. But if that was found in my drawer—"

"When did you find it?"

"A few moments ago. I did not know what to do. So I brought it to you."

"Which is your room?"

"The first in the passage, on the other side. Brother Anselm's."

"When did you last look at the place where you found it?"

"After dinner. I went to tidy up and get a handkerchief before going to the TV. It was not there then."

"You are sure of that?"

"Quite sure."

"Your door was not locked?"

"Of course not. Is that the weapon that shot hint?"

Roger picked it up in his handkerchief and opened it.

"It might well be," he said. "From the smell it has recently been used. Three shots are gone and two left. Ewen apparently had two. Whether they are identical with these the experts will tell us. Your idea is that someone shot him with this and then hid it in your drawer?"

"It must have been."

Fear was in her eyes. It certainly looked that way. But, if she had done the shooting, to hand the gun over with such a story would be a good way of getting rid of it before there was further search. That must be borne in mind. In any event it seemed to dispose of the theory of the outsider from the village.

"Tell me, Miss Wren—"

"Call me Gwen. Everyone does. It is not so policeman-like."

"Tell me, Gwen, what were your relations with Ewen Jones?"

She hesitated. Then she looked straight at him and said quietly, "You know I had been living with him?"

"He told me so. Had you thought of marrying?"

"Not really. We liked one another well enough, but we differed a good deal. We both knew it would not work. It was more likely to last if we were free to end it, if you can understand that."

"Did he tell you I wanted him to give up the house?"

"He did. He was not sure what he meant to do about it. But if he went I think he meant us to part."

"What were your feelings for him when you came down here?"

"I liked him, as I always did. We had a lot of fun together. I didn't really want to come. It meant putting up a show before his people, but he persuaded me. Then he treated me like that."

"Like what exactly?"

"He had told me he meant to talk about the abolition of the Monarchy. I said it would be crazy. But he did it—more to spite me then because he believed in it. He hardly spoke to me when I got here. He was all the time running after Sandra—"

"Was that why you played that trick with her bathing costume?"

For the first time Gwen showed something of a smile, not a kind smile.

"It was a chance not to miss. If she was stealing my man did it not serve her right?"

"You would have left her in the hut, perhaps to take a chill?"

"Cooling down was good for her. I did get a wrap but there was no hurry for it. She could have come in if she wanted to. Everyone would have laughed at her—except perhaps Ossie and Ewen."

"Does Ossie love her?"

"Who can tell? He gave Ewen every opportunity to be with her."

"That annoyed you?"

"Was it not natural? He insisted on my coming and then he never noticed me, but devoted himself to her. Had he told me straightforwardly it was all over with us I would not have minded so much. It was the way he did it. I can look after myself. I earn as much as he does. It was such a slap in the face."

There was another pause. Then Roger said, "Whose idea was it that you should all four be in Sandra's room last night?"

"I don't think it was anyone's idea. It was a mix-up. I went there with Sandra because I wondered if Ewen would have the nerve to do so. But she seemed to want me to stay."

"What did you talk about?"

"Mostly my newspaper and magazine work. I told her I once met Princess Margaret and I had covered the Townsend story when everyone was so excited about it. She asked a lot of questions. Then Ewen came. He looked sick at finding me there and didn't know what to say. Ossie came immediately after and muttered something about his toothbrush. No one believed him. Then the party ended."

"That is all you can tell me about it?"

"That is there was."

"Someone shot Ewen. Was Ossie jealous of him?"

Gwen shrugged. "He had reason to be, but he had not shown it before."

"Can you suggest anyone else who might have shot him? Had Ewen any real enemy among the people who were here? You must know how they felt for one another."

Gwen considered the question for some moments. Her earlier agitation had passed.

"There is a lot of jealousy among M.P.s. They are like actors wanting the limelight, though Ewen was generally popular. In the Unions there is rivalry to become a District Secretary or a Regional Organiser. And, of course, there is the National Executive where there is likely to be a vacancy soon. I believe Ruttle and Gibbons both have hopes in that direction."

"Had Ewen?"

"If he had he was going the wrong way about it.'

"Would Ruttle or Gibbons have regarded him as a serious rival?"

"Possibly. But it is a matter of intrigue, not murder!"

"And we have to find a murderer." She made no reply.

"Who knew which was your room?"

"Everyone in the corridor, I expect."

"How many knew of your affair with Ewen?"

She answered more slowly. "I never told anyone and I don't think he did. Some may have guessed, though we were both busy with our work and I kept a room at my club."

"It is important. What I want to get at is this: did the person who, as you say, put this weapon in your room do so because he was aware of your association with Ewen and sensed there was something of a quarrel, or was it because he was in a hurry and yours was the first room he came to?"

She shook her head. "Your guess is as good as mine."

"Is there anything else you can tell me?"

"Nothing. I was still fond of him. I still thought he would need me. I—I hope you will find who did it."

There was a break in her voice. He stood up.

"I hope that too, Gwen. You understand I must tell the police all you have told me. They will want to question you about it. I must hand them this weapon and if the shots tally they will test it for finger-prints. They will, of course, find yours but we will hope there are others as well. Good night."

He opened the door and glanced along the passage. It was deserted.

"Thank you a lot," she whispered. "I feel better now I have told you."

He watched her as she went swiftly and silently to her own room. As she entered it he thought he heard another door close. The light was dim and he could not tell which it was. He walked quickly after her but except for hers there was no glimmer under any of the doors.

12

"As He was Ambitious I Slew Him"

Roger was pleased when he heard in the morning that Scotland Yard were sending Superintendent Yeo and Inspector Allenby to take over the case. He had worked with them before and they were both good men. It also showed the serious view that head quarters took of the matter.

Unlike the previous day, everyone except Lord and Lady Bethesda came down to breakfast. Several admitted to a restless night. Never before had they come into such close contact with a murder and all were anxious to know if there had been any fresh developments in the affair. Some were asking how soon they could get away.

Before joining them at the table Roger went outside to see by day the windows between which the shots had presumably been fired. A local constable was on guard, a relief for the man who had been positioned there the night before.

Roger had seen the tall, heavy casements from the inside and there was no special feature about them from without. They came down to about two feet from the ground. In front of them was the flower-bed, a yard or so in width. All the blossoms had been beaten down by the torrential rain but some of the stalks were broken, probably by being trodden on. There was no question of identifying footmarks as both the path and the border had been literally flooded.

Turning over the broken blossoms with a stick Roger noticed a scrap of paper hidden among them.

"What is that?" he asked.

"Dunno, sir," the constable said. "I was told not to touch anything nor to let no one else touch anything."

The man did not know him and Roger thought it better not to disobey instructions.

"Superintendent Yeo from Scotland Yard will be along soon," he said. "Keep a special eye on that paper till he comes. It might be important."

He then went in to get some breakfast. Most of those already there murmured good morning and several asked if he had heard anything fresh. To which he said he had not. He noticed that Bill Ruttle was making a good meal and Fred Gibbons was not needing to force himself to eat. Sandra had moved from beside the vacant chair that had been Ewen's and was seated some way off, but was not with her husband. Gwennie Wren was drinking tea but eating little. Rhoda smiled wanly at him but did not speak.

"I understand our meeting is off" Ruttle remarked. "There is nothing for us to stay for."

"I would not say that," Roger replied. "Men from Scotland Yard are on the way. They will probably want to ask us all a few questions."

"Not very pleasant to stay in a home where a thing like this has happened," Ruttle returned.

"Major Bennion is right," Gibbons said. "It would look odd if we ran away. We must say what we know and help if we can."

"No question of running away," Ruttle muttered. "We told all we could to that inspector fellow last night. At least I did. Isn't that good enough?"

"I believe your meeting was for this afternoon," Roger said. "You were all staying until then, or to the morning."

"My wife and I were meaning to go to the service at the local church," Mr. Dayton remarked. "I suppose that will be all right?"

Roger knew he could vouch for "Jeremiah" but deemed it unwise to appear to show partiality. "I think it better not. The constables have orders to stop anyone leaving the house. The Yard men should be here very soon."

There were faint grumbles from some of the men but their wives were content. Curiosity may have played a part or they might have disliked the idea of returning home with no meal prepared.

"How are your uncle and aunt this morning?" Roger asked Rhoda. "Have you seen them?"

"Yes," she said. "Uncle had a poor night. Aunt Connie thinks he had better stay in bed. She will be down presently to see to things."

"And your little friend, Master Ambrose?"

"He is all right. We have not told him anything yet." She paused then added, "Isn't it horrible? Will these people be able to clear it up? I could hardly sleep for thinking of it. It seems so incredible. Ewen was so full of life, so happy."

She looked pale and there was a sob in her voice.

"It is horrible, my dear," he said gently. "We must all help to clear it up as quickly as we can."

Then there was the sound of a car in the drive. The men from the Yard had arrived. He went to meet them. Superintendent Yeo and Inspector Allenby jumped out. So did a third man, introduced as Sergeant Carston.

"Nice to meet you again, Major Bennion," Yeo said, shaking his hand. "A bit odd though that when we arrive at the scene of a murder we find you there. The third time, isn't it? Rather suspicious!"

"All right," Roger returned. "I'll come quietly. But first I want to show you something."

He led the way round the house to the window of the television room.

"We think the shots were fired from here," he said. "I am curious about that scrap of paper. It might of course have blown out of the window; it might have been there for a long time; or it might have fallen from the murderer's pocket. The constable did not want me to touch it. If you prefer not to tread on the flower-bed we could easily reach it from the inside."

"That is the best way," Yeo said. "I have the key to the room. Bellairs locked it last night and gave it to me. He will be along presently."

They entered the house. The TV room was in some disorder as it had not been touched since the tragedy. The only signs of that were the spots of blood on and beside the chair where Ewen Jones had died.

"The window-frame and the sill have yet to be tested for finger-prints," Roger said. "Be careful about that."

It was, however, easy for a tall man like Allenby to lean over the sill and pick up the paper. He handed it to Yeo. It appeared to be a half-sheet of ordinary notepaper folded in two, though still damp from the rain that had fallen on it. On the inner side were a few typewritten words slightly blurred and all in capitals—AS HE WAS AMBITIOUS I SLEW HIM.

They all stared at it.

"Those words seem familiar," Yeo muttered.

"As he was valiant I honour him, but as he was ambitious I slew him," Roger quoted. "It is a from the oration by Brutus at the death of Julius Caesar."

"Was Ewen Jones ambitious?" Yeo asked.

"I suppose all politicians are, more or less." Roger replied.

"According to Bellairs there was a party of politicians here, Members and their wives," the superintendent said. "He spent a good part of the night writing his report. I have only had time to glance through it, but he told me you were at their meeting."

"That is so, but before we go into that there is something else I have to show you. I think we might take possession of the study."

He led the way to the room where Bill Ruttle said he had spent the previous evening. On a desk there was stout, crested note paper ready for use, but it was of a quality superior to the sodden scrap they had found.

"You ought to have this," Roger said. He handed over the snub-nosed revolver he had received from Gwennie Wren. "It may be the weapon that was used."

"How did you get it?"

Roger told him. He said they were all rather late in going to bed after the shock of the discovery of the crime and after the questioning by Bellairs. "It was about one o'clock when Miss Wren brought it to me. She told me had just found it, partially hidden among her clothes. The suggestion was that the person who used it put it there, possibly to incriminate her, possibly only to get rid of it."

"Bellairs gave me the chart you made of the seats occupied by the people in the TV room," Yeo said. He produced and studied it. "Gwennie Wren was at the end of the third row. If that is right and no one left the room during the play she could not have shot the man and also dropped the note in the garden."

"That is so," Roger agreed, "but we do not know how long the note had been there. If the crime was premeditated it could have been put among the flowers before. There is another point you ought to know. Gwen and Ewen had been living together for some time and appear to have quarrelled. I told her I must inform you and that you would probably want a statement from her."

"I certainly shall, but before I see any of them I would like you to describe the party. It seems quite a mixed bag. How, for instance, did you happen to be here?"

"Quite a story," Roger said. "Have you ever heard of Old Nick's Folly in the East-end of London?"

"I have," Allenby said. "A bright oasis in a desert of grime. It was once on my beat."

"It belongs to my father. He built it as a sort of charity to give pleasant homes to aged and deserving people at nominal rents. By something of a trick Ewen Jones got one of them. You know how difficult it is to get rid of tenants in these days.'

"Was Gwennie Wren there with him?" Yeo asked.

"She was. I do not know how often or for how long. By an odd coincidence we had an application for a cottage there irons Dan Floss, gardener here to Lord Bethesda. I suggested to Ewen that he should go and let Floss have it."

"Did he agree?"

"He did not. He suggested I should come to this party and try to persuade his father to make him an allowance towards another home. I said politics were not in my line, but he was quite keen on it. His plan was very hush-hush and if a few non-political people were present it might pass as an ordinary house-party. He also promised me some fishing, so I came. I did mention the matter to Lord Bethesda. It appeared to shock him that his son was living to some extent on charity and he said he must go. He made no promise of financial aid but he was anxious to get rid of Floss who is past work. He wants his cottage for another gardener."

"Does Floss know of this?"

"I saw him soon after I got here and told him how matters stood. I have not seen him since, but last night in describing his walk in the garden Captain Henshaw said he had seen a man lurking out there who might have been a gardener. Would it save time if Allenby asked Floss as to his movements?"

"It would. Floss was promised the cottage if Ewen went, so he made sure of his going! Is that it?"

"It is a possibility," Roger said. "I do not think Floss, with his twisted fingers, could type that message. I am not even sure he could fire a gun. It might check Henshaw's statement."

Allenby left them. Yeo said, "Tell me something of the political side of the affair."

"Ewen told me he was trying to form a Ginger Group to make the Labour people more Socialistic. We mostly arrived on Friday and after dinner that night Lord Bethesda suggested that his son should outline the proposals to be put before the bigger meeting here today."

"What were they?"

"Somewhat incoherent. He asked for the abolition of all hereditary titles, including the Monarchy. He wanted some rather startling financial reforms in order to pay off or reduce the National Debt, but his real object seemed to be changes in the Trade Unions by which there could be no strikes without the permission of a new Grand Council who would enforce the demands by a strike of not one trade but of every trade. So whether there was a Labour Government or a Tory Government that Grand Council would virtually rule the country. That is perhaps the most important point as nearly all the members present are Trade Union nominees."

"More important than the abolition of the Monarchy?" Yeo asked.

"Only from our immediate angle. Someone asked who would be on the Grand Council and who would be its chairman, a sort of Stalin they called him."

"What did Ewen say?"

"The Council would be elected, but for chairman he suggested his father. Lord Bethesda at once disclaimed the idea. If it was to be, they must look for a younger man such as his son."

"How was that taken?"

"Ewen looked a little gratified, I thought. But he brushed it aside and went on to something else."

"But is that what he was really after? Some ambition! So I slew him! He had a rival for the job. How was the proposal taken?"

"It had a mixed reception, but later on they all seemed to agree he was a jolly good fellow. There is however another angle you must consider, quite different. Ewen was paying very marked attentions to Sandra, Henshaw's wife."

"I thought it was Ewen and Gwennie Wren?"

"It had been," Roger said, "but Ewen neglected her for Sandra. Henshaw is the only one who owns to being in the garden last night. He could hardly deny it as some time after playing billiards with me he came in, soaking wet. Bellairs and I met him. He said he had been caught in the storm and had taken refuge in a hut beside the river."

"He would not have called Ewen ambitious," Yeo remarked.

"Why not? A man might think it very ambitious of another man to seek to entice his wife. Apart from that, if for any reason you wished to shoot a politician you knew to be ambitious, might you not plant such a note near him to put the scent on a false trail?"

"You certainly might. There is no shortage of motives, quite a nice choice. Henshaw was jealous of Ewen for his attentions to Sandra. Gwennie Wren was jealous for the same reason and any of the M.P.s may have resented his ambitions. Floss wanted his house. Take your choice! Did Bellairs, by the way, search Henshaw for a weapon?"

"He did not. It did occur to me, but my idea at the moment was that he got wet taking it to the river to dispose of it."

"This is easily concealed," Yeo said, pointing to the revolver. "Bellairs reports that Henshaw went up to change. He could then have put it in Gwen's room as she and everyone else was downstairs. Who should we see first?"

"I would like you to meet Rhoda Rees. She is Bethesda's niece and also his secretary. She did a good deal in arranging the whole affair. She, of course, has a typewriter."

"Ewen was her cousin. What was her feeling for him?"

"Only cousinly. But you can ask her."

13

Where is Angela?

Rhoda had a strained look. She was wearing a simple black frock and she at once took the seat Roger offered her. He introduced Yeo and tried to reassure her.

"This is Superintendent Yeo of Scotland Yard, but he is not really as terrifying as that sounds. He wants to ask you a few questions."

"You lead off," Yeo said, eyeing the girl carefully.

"Well, Rhoda," Roger began, "which is your room, I mean your working-room?"

"The next one to this," she said a little shyly.

"Did any of your visitors come there to you?"

"Several of them."

"Can you remember which?"

She considered for a moment. "Captain Henshaw, Mrs. Doodell, Miss Wren, Mr. Ruttle, Mr. Edmonds, Mr. Gibbons—my door was generally open unless I was busy. I had asked them to come to me if they wanted anything."

"Most of them, in fact, came. Was it for any particular purpose or just for a little chat?"

"They generally asked questions about my uncle and aunt and how we ordinarily lived. Mr. Dayton wanted to know where our church was and Mr. Ruttle asked if I would type some notes for him. I said I would, but he never brought them."

"You, of course, have a typewriter. Have you any paper like this?" He showed her the sheet they had found, with the words downwards.

"I don't think so. Has this been in the rain?"

"I believe it has," Roger said. "Rather cheap, isn't it—might have been the back half of a letter?"

"Very likely."

"Could your typewriter have typed this?"

He turned it over and she read the ominous words "As he was ambitious I slew him."

"It certainly might have done. Here is a little break in the top of the S like mine has, and the B is not quite perfect. It is an old machine."

"You did not type it?"

"No."

"Or anyone else to your knowledge?"

"No."

Yeo intervened. "As your machine is in the next room let us see you type the same words underneath those."

She led the way to her room, plainly furnished as a neatly-kept office. She slipped the paper into her elderly Oliver and typed the same words, also in capitals. There was no doubt of it. The spacing and the slight defects were identical. That line had been typed on her machine.

"I suppose anyone with a very small knowledge of typing could have done it in a minute or two," Yeo asked, "possibly with one finger?"

"Oh, yes."

"Do you know if anyone here does typing?"

"Miss Wren does," Rhoda said. "She has a portable and showed it me. She is a writer, you know. It is a new model and the type is quite different."

Yeo made no comment and they returned to the room they had left.

"Any idea, Rhoda, what the words mean?" Roger asked.

"Is it a quotation from Shakespeare's Julius Caesar?"

"I believe it is. Would you say Ewen was ambitious?"

She seemed to realise something of the implications, but she answered steadily. "Every good man is if he wants to get on, isn't he?"

"What did you think of his speech on Friday night?"

"As I told you, I had heard some of it before. But not what he said about the Queen. I did not like that."

"You were late in the TV room last night. Had you been in the garden?"

"Yes."

"Meeting someone?" he smiled.

"Yes." She blushed a little.

"Jeremy, of course. Not to be confused with our Jeremiah—Mr. Dayton. Did you see anyone besides Jeremy while you were out there? Near the window of the TV room, perhaps?"

"No one at all. We were in the front of the house."

"Just one thing more, Rhoda. The first time I saw you and Jeremy you were outside that hut at the end of the garden. You went away and almost immediately afterwards Captain and Mrs. Henshaw emerged from it, looking as if they had been quarrelling. Had you heard what they were saying?"

She looked uncomfortable. "A little," she said. "Jerry heard more and told me. I would sooner you asked him. I have not seen him since—since last night. I meant to ask him to tell you, but I cannot believe it is true."

"Who is Jerry or Jeremy?" Yeo asked.

"Jeremy Valiance, the village schoolmaster," she said.

"Jeremy and Rhoda are engaged," Roger told him. "It is a secret and must be regarded as confidential." He wanted Yeo to have the facts and also thought it wise to correct any ideas he might have as to the girl's feeling for her cousin.

"You think what you heard may be important, but you would rather we got it from him?" Yeo asked.

"Yes, please."

"How soon can we get him?"

She glanced at her wrist watch. "Almost at once. It is nearly time for the break. I will telephone him, but don't keep him long."

"Don't telephone," the superintendent said. "I will send for him with the car. That will be quicker."

"Thank you, Rhoda," Roger smiled. "You have helped us quite a lot. Tell Sergeant Carston where to go."

He opened the door and she and the sergeant went out. The latter was a shorthand expert and had been taking notes unobtrusively of what he heard.

As they left, Allenby came in. He was carrying a gun of some sort which he placed on the table.

"I have seen Floss," he said. "He admits he was in the garden last night, so Henshaw might have seen him. His story is that he was worrying about his chance of setting that cottage in London and wandered to the house hoping he might see Major Bennion. Everything was quiet and he saw no one until Henshaw came out. He was not perfectly sure who he was; it was at a distance and very dark, but it was not Ewen. He thought it might seem queer if he was seen hanging about at that time of night and he smelt rain coming so he went back to his own place. A crabby old chap, but he seemed straightforward."

"What about his gun?" Yeo asked.

"I saw it in the corner of his room. A rook rifle. Noticing his deformed fingers I wondered if he could still use it. He said he had shot a bird with it early this morning and proud of the fact. I asked how he could load it. He showed me. A slow and clumsy business, but he did it. If Ewen Jones had two or more shots in him I do not think Floss fired them. The gun only takes one at a time and to fumble a reload in the dark would hardly be possible for him. I thought it best to bring it along and some of the cartridges to compare with what the doctor finds in the body."

"Quite right," said Yeo.

"I do not think Floss is our man," Roger remarked. "Apart from anything else I fancy he would wait until he heard from me. Also, I doubt if he would have known exactly where Ewen was sitting. A rook rifle could perhaps have done it, so as there was one it is as well to know who had it at the time."

"That is not all," Allenby said with the air of one who has kept the best till the last. "Floss told me he saw a second man."

"You said he only saw one man," Yeo interrupted.

"He only saw one man come out of the house, probably Henshaw. This was later, as he was going home. A short, stout fellow. He might have been a guest but he thought he knew him. Not being sure he was unwilling to say much; but I eventually got it from Mrs. Floss, as he had told her the night before. It was an odd-job man from the village, Luke Catling. He does house repairs in a small way. He has a pretty daughter named Angela and Ewen Jones had been interested in her."

"Quite a new line," Yeo said. "What else?"

"Nothing, sir. Floss interrupted his wife and told her no scandal must be talked. After that I could get no more from either of them. I went to the village and found Luke Catling. When I questioned him, he admitted he was in the garden last night. I thought you might like to see him so I brought him along."

"Good. Bring him in. It may save troubling other people."

"Short and stout might describe Gibbons," Roger said, as Allenby went to fetch his man, "but if it is a matter of village scandal I can understand old Floss not wishing to be concerned. He might think it would prejudice his chance of getting Ewen's cottage."

Luke Catling was a thick-set fellow as described, rather swarthy in appearance. He did not give the impression of being very intelligent, though he might be cunning. He was holding his cloth cap in his hand and seemed rather scared at the position in which he found himself.

"You were in the garden here last night," Yeo began abruptly.

"Yes, sir."

"At what time?"

"Doan know 'zac'ly. Might've been about 'arf past eight."

"Why did you come through the garden?"

"No, sir, not 'zac'ly. I coom through trade entrance, like I allus did. Done jobs 'ere, I 'ave."

"Then how did you get into the garden?"

"I walked round."

"Why did you come?"

"I—I wanted to see Mister Ewen."

"You went to the trade door?"

"No, sir. Through the kitchen windy I seed some strange men, like butlers, so I thought I better 'adn't. I went round to the garden in case Mister Ewen were there."

"And then?"

"I seed they were in the televisin' room. Leastwise I 'eard 'em. I knew 'e wouldn't want to be disturbed like, so I come 'ome."

"Did you see anyone at all?"

"Only old Floss. Leastwise I thought it was 'im. 'E was some way off and it was purty dark."

"Now, Catling," Yeo said, "tell me why you wanted to see Mr. Ewen?"

So far the man had stood up to his questioning very well. But at this he twisted his cap in his hands and his reply was slow in coming.

"I just wanted to see 'im."

"You know what happened to him last night?"

"I—not 'zac'ly, sir. There's been talk in the village."

"He was shot. Have you a gun, Catling?"

"Me? No, sir. 'Aven't 'andled one since I were in the army, and not often then. I was a norderly. Never went overseas."

"I believe you have a daughter—Angela?"

"Yes, sir." Luke hesitated a moment and then thrust his hand into his breast pocket and took out a rather shabby photograph. "That's 'er, sir."

Yeo and Roger examined it. It showed a girl of a gipsy type in a Zingari dancing costume. Dark like her father and decidedly good-looking.

"You wished to see Mr. Ewen about her?"

"Yes, sir."

"Why?"

The fellow hesitated. Then he told his story.

"Mr. Ewen seed 'er at a dancin' show we 'ad in the village 'all about two months ago. Mad on dancin' she were. 'E spoke to 'er and said if she ever coom to Lonnon she must let 'im know and most likely 'e could get 'er a job. 'E gave 'er the address to write to. Then she disappeared."

"How do you mean she disappeared?"

"She went off a few days later and said we'd 'ear from 'er when she was famous. But we never 'eard a word. Not that she was ever one for writin' letters. But I thought Mister Ewen could tell us where she were. There was a lady with 'im at the time and she said she might 'elp 'er too. The neighbours got a talkin' and when I 'eard Mister Ewen was 'ere, 'e doan orfen come, I thought I'd ask 'im about 'er."

"Can you describe the lady?" Roger asked. "The one who said she might help."

"I did see 'er, sir. She were dark, like our Angela. She's been 'ere afore. Angela said 'e called 'er Gwen."

That was important. It was not impossible that Ewen would have taken Gwennie Wren with him to a local show if she was staying there at the time. She might corroborate the story, though if he had any designs on this girl would he have furthered them in her presence?

"You do not know that Angela in fact went to London?" Roger said.

"She told us she were goin' there."

"Had you the address?"

He shook his head. "Er never told us."

"You could easily have got Mr. Ewen's address, or written to him here?"

"Didn't think o' that."

"Angela is a pretty girl. She must have had many admirers."

"Plenty of 'em," Luke grinned, "but none good enough for 'er."

"You do not know for a fact that she went to Mr. Ewen?"

The man's mean little eyes tried to look bolder.

"Must've done. Others 'eard him ask 'er. That's what made the neighbours talk and my wife said I must see 'im when 'e coom agen. O' course I doan want to make trouble. I only want my little gel."

"You do not seem to have been in any hurry about it," Yeo said sharply. "I will keep the photograph. May help us to trace her. That's all. You can go now but I may have to see you again."

"I doan want to make trouble," the handy-man repeated as he shuffled to the door. "I only wants to know 'er is all right and wot 'e did with 'er."

"What do you make of that?" Yeo enquired when he had gone. "If true it shows Ewen Jones in a new light."

"I doubt if Catling did the shooting," Roger said. "I doubt if he could

91

use the typewriter and quote that bit of Shakespeare. I doubt if he could have gone upstairs and put the gun in Gwen's room. There may be something in the story, even if it is mainly local gossip. I should say he is not above a bit of blackmail and hearing of Ewen's death wondered if there was anything in it for him."

Then Rhoda came in and said Lady Bethesda was down and was at liberty if they wished to see her.

"Please ask her to come," Yeo replied.

Lady Bethesda was dressed in black. She appeared severely composed and took the chair she was offered. Yeo murmured some words of sympathy and asked how her husband was bearing up after the shock.

"His lordship is a very sick man," she said. "I doubt if he will be allowed up today, but the doctor will be along soon. Probably I can tell you all he could."

Yeo again expressed his regret. He might have to see Lord Bethesda later but would certainly spare him as much as possible.

"Whose idea was it to have this party?" he asked.

"Mr. Ewen's. I did not like the idea but his father thought it his duty to agree to it."

'Did you know the people who were coming?"

"I did not," was the icy reply. "With the exception of Captain and Mrs. Henshaw and Miss Wren, I have never met any of them before. They came as Mr. Ewen's guests."

"Did you or his lordship know what he meant to say to them?"

"We did not or we should not have permitted it here."

"I take it you disapproved of it?"

"Of a great deal of it."

"Did it indicate personal ambition on his part?"

She considered for a few moments. "Not as he put it."

"Would you say he was ambitious?"

Her reply was more tart. "That is hardly the word I should use. Irresponsible might express it better. These young men have wild ideas until they grow out of them. I was fond of Ewen but I wanted him to grow up."

"As he invited these people it is difficult to think he would bring anyone who might wish to kill him?"

"Is it?" she rejoined. "If one of them was ambitious—to use your word—he might think Ewen stood in his way for promotion. I do not trust Socialists. They killed one another in plenty at the time of the French Revolution. They still do in Russia."

Yeo did not comment on that. He produced Roger's chart of the seats on the previous night.

"This shows how the people were sitting at the time when Ewen was shot. Would you say it is correct?"

She glanced at it. "It appears to be, but provided they all found seats I was not interested. There was plenty of room."

"You and Lord Bethesda occupied these two seats nearest the door?"

"We did."

"Do you think anyone could have entered or gone out during the play without your knowing it?"

"Our attention was on the screen but I think it unlikely."

"So far as you know no one did?"

"Rhoda, my niece, came in a little late. That is all I can tell you."

"If the shots came from the garden that would exempt all who were in the room?"

"I think so."

"Naturally you do not know what the guests who were not in the room were doing. That we must get from them. What of your domestic staff?"

"They all have good characters," she said a little haughtily. "The inspector questioned them last night and I believe was satisfied."

"All old servants?"

"No. Some are here only for the weekend but they all have excellent credentials. You can, of course, check them."

"Thank you, Lady Bethesda. We may have to do that. Was Mr. Ewen popular in the village?"

"Hardly popular; he was seldom here."

"He could have had no clandestine affair with any girl in the village?"

"I should certainly hope not," was the chilly reply. "I never heard of such a thing. I trust he had too much self-esteem and respect for us for that."

"So far as you are aware he had no entanglements here or elsewhere?"

"So far as I am aware he had not, but we knew little of his life in London where he spent most of his time."

"You cannot suggest anything that will help me?"

"I regret I cannot. Ewen filled the house with strangers. It is very unpleasant."

They all rose as she went out.

"Very unpleasant," Yeo repeated. "She does not seem overwhelmed with grief at her son's death."

"Her stepson," Roger corrected. "I do not think there was any great affection on either side."

"Too much My Lady to be emotional," Inspector Allenby commented. He had been present all the time, taking the necessary notes. He still had his suspicions about his own find, Luke Catling.

Then a car drew up and Sergeant Carston alighted with a young man. They entered the room together.

Jeremy Valiance was a pleasant-looking fellow about twenty-five years of age. He wore a tweed jacket and grey trousers; more of a sporting type than a scholar. As he had played cricket for his college and had graduated creditably he no doubt had all-round qualifications for his present job and might hope for something better.

Yeo soon got to business. After a few preliminary questions he asked, "You are acquainted with Miss Rhoda Rees?"

"I am. May I see her?"

"Fetch her," Yeo said to the sergeant, after a moment's consideration.

That did not take long as she had heard the car arrive and was waiting near the door. The two smiled at one another and sat down side by side.

"When did you hear of Ewen Jones's murder?" Yeo addressed Jeremy.

"It was rumoured round the village this morning. I meant to come to make enquiries as soon as I was free."

"You were a friend if his?"

"I had met him a few times. I did not know him well."

"Are you a Socialist?"

Jeremy smiled. "That depends on your definition of Socialism. I regard myself as an Independent. I believe in levelling up rather than levelling down. Better education and equal opportunities for those willing to avail themselves of them."

"Do you hold with Ewen's views?"

"If you mean those he expressed at that dinner, I do not."

"How do you know of them?" Yeo asked sharply.

"Rhoda told me."

"Hm. Over to you, Major Bennion."

"Hello, Jeremy, if I may call you that," Roger said pleasantly, "I believe you and Rhoda hope some day to marry?"

"That is so, sir." Rhoda slipped her hand in his.

"Lord and Lady Bethesda do not approve?"

"We intend to marry. They do not know that yet."

"I understand. We were all young once, even policemen. Where did you and Rhoda generally meet?"

"It depended on when she was free and for how long. If I had not seen her during the day I generally cycled to the front drive and waited for her. She slipped out if she could for a few minutes."

"But on Friday afternoon?"

"I waited for her in the hut by the river. That is our favourite walk."

"I was making for the river," Roger said, "and I thought I saw you together outside the hut. Will you tell us about that?"

"We met at the hut and walked a little way. Then Rhoda thought she had dropped a scarf there and we went back for it. We heard people talking inside and waited for them to go."

95

"Who were they?"

"I did not see them. There seemed to be a man and a woman."

"Did you hear what they were saying?"

"We could not help hearing some of it. They were quarrelling."

"What did you hear? Please be as precise as you can."

"At first they spoke softly, but I heard Ewen's name. Then the woman said 'I refuse to go on with it. It is caddish'. I could not catch what the man said, but she replied 'If I do I shall stick to him'. Then the man said angrily 'If you do I will shoot him'."

"You are sure he used those words—'I will shoot him'?"

"Quite sure."

"Anything else?"

"No. Rhoda beckoned me and I left with her."

"Well, Rhoda," Roger said turning, "how much of this did you hear?"

"Only the first part. They were quarrelling about Ewen. I did not want to listen and I turned away. Then I saw you coming and I beckoned to Jeremy and we went down again through the woods."

"Did you hear the threat to shoot Ewen?"

"No. Jeremy told me that. When—when he was shot—I knew he must tell you."

"You did not know who the man and woman were, Jeremy?"

"Not then. When we walked away Rhoda told me they were Captain and Mrs. Henshaw."

"You were sure of that?" Yeo asked Rhoda. He had been listening intently to all that was said.

"There is no doubt of it," Roger answered for her. "I saw Rhoda and Jeremy beside the hut and as they went away the Henshaws came out. Probably they had seen me through the open door. I spoke to them. He had his rod and said he had caught nothing. He seemed out of temper. I thought that was the reason."

"The next day Ewen was shot!" Yeo muttered. "When did you young people meet again?"

"Last night, soon after eight," Jeremy answered. "I had found Rhoda's scarf and brought it back to her."

"What sort of scarf is it?"

"Green tartan," Rhoda said.

"Where did this happen?"

"I was at the end of the drive at eight," Jeremy said. "Rhoda came a few minutes later."

"How long were you together?"

"Not long. She said she had to go to the TV show."

"That is why she got in after it had started," Roger commented. "What did you do when she had gone?"

"I cycled home."

"What time did you get there?"

"I cannot say exactly," Jeremy replied. "Well before the storm broke. My sister can confirm that."

"Had you a gun with you?" Superintendent Yeo asked.

"I do not own a gun," Jeremy said.

"I did not ask that. I said had you a gun?"

"I had not."

"Did you see anyone in the garden?"

"I did not go into the garden; my cycle was just inside the drive gates and I went home."

"It was then, I suppose, that Rhoda told you of Ewen's speech the night before?" Roger remarked.

"It was."

"I only told him the bits about the Queen and the Supreme Trade Council," Rhoda said.

"And you disapproved?" Roger asked him.

"I disapproved most strongly. I thought about it as I cycled back. The Queen is the finest woman in the land, perhaps in the world. You cannot imagine the people of the Commonwealth coming out in their tens of thousands, women and children as well as men, to see a President go by, whether he was an Attlee or a Gaitskell, or even

Winston Churchill. As to Trade Unions, I approve of them but not when they become tyrants and a man can be sent to Coventry because he honours his obligations as well as he can."

Jeremy spoke warmly and looked from Roger to Yeo.

"We will not discuss that," the latter said. "Do you know a girl in the village called Angela Catling?"

"I do, or rather did."

"Did you ever hear her name coupled with Mr. Ewen?"

Jeremy hesitated. "I do not quite know what you mean. She was an attractive girl in a way and wanted to go to London to become a dancer. It was reported that Mr. Ewen said if she did go he might be able to help her."

"She went to London?"

"She left the village. I know no more than that."

"You know her father, Luke Catling. What can you tell us about him?"

"He does odd jobs for various people. A bit of a scrounger in my opinion."

"Of a criminal type?"

"In a petty way, perhaps."

"Do you know anything about Angela, Rhoda?" Roger enquired.

"Only what Jeremy has told you. Of course I knew her as a village girl, rather a flighty one perhaps."

"Attractive to Ewen?"

"Oh no, not at all."

"That will do for the present," Yeo said. "What you have told us may be of assistance. It shall be typed out for you to sign, if it is correct."

14

Sandra's Story

"It begins to add up," Roger said when the young couple had left them.

"You believe this story?" Yeo asked. "The Henshaws quarrelled about Ewen Jones who was paying attentions to the wife, and the husband shot him as he had threatened?"

"It could be so, though that was not what I meant."

"You suspect Jeremy Valiance, who was left alone in the garden at the critical time?" Allenby suggested. "There is no evidence when he cycled home."

"His sister," Yeo said.

"We have not seen her," Allenby pointed out. "He could tell her what to say."

"How would he put the gun—if he had one—in Miss Wren's room?" Roger queried. "What is his motive?"

"He might resent the attack on the Queen," Yeo commented, "like the men who slew Becket in the cathedral to please their King. But I cannot see it that way."

"Nor can I," Roger said. "The vapourings of Master Ewen were not important enough for that. I only meant it made sense of a queer affair in Sandra's bedroom the first night I was here. I happen to know her husband is very hard up. I suggest we should see her next."

"Get her," Yeo bade Allenby.

Sandra had taken care over her toilet and looked really beautiful. Her blue eyes were a little sad but her golden hair was very becomingly arranged. She was wearing a grey pullover that revealed the shape of her fine figure and a dark skirt. Probably the nearest approach to mourning in the limited wardrobe she had brought with her. There were no rings on her fingers, not even a wedding ring. That was curious, especially in a company largely of married women. Could it be an oversight or was it intentional? When she was seated Yeo began abruptly.

99

"Mrs. Henshaw, would you say Ewen Jones was ambitious?"

If he thought the word would disconcert her he was disappointed. She replied rather as Rhoda had done to the same question.

"Ambitious? I suppose he was, in a way. All men should desire to make good in their particular line."

"Can you use a typewriter?" This again was abrupt. Her only reaction was of surprise.

"Are you offering me a job? I thought of learning when I was young but I gave it up."

Yeo did not reply. "Over to you, Bennion," he said.

Roger began in his usual friendly way.

"Sandra, we want to ask you a few questions, but as they may concern your husband you are entitled to refuse to answer them."

"No harm in asking," she said coolly.

"Thank you. I believe you and he arrived here before the rest of the party. When was it?"

"Last Wednesday. We were invited for a week. The party did not concern us. We were not interested in the political wrangle."

"You were Ewen's guests?"

"Surely we were Lady Bethesda's guests? Actually Ewen asked us, as he had done before."

"Am I right in saying Ewen paid you a good deal of attention?"

"Would it not be his duty to do so?"

"Did your husband disapprove?"

"That you must ask him," Sandra said with a slightly mocking smile.

"I arrived on Friday," Roger went on. "You were given one of the single rooms opposite mine in the Monks' corridor?"

"I did not know where your room was. To be quite candid, I was not interested."

"Thank you. But you did not share your husband's room?"

"I did not. Rhoda told us they were short of double rooms with so many people coming, so we offered to take single ones. There were plenty of them, as befitted the monastic life."

"When you retired that night Gwennie Wren came with you and talked outside my door for some while. Then you entered your room together. Whose suggestion was that?"

"Have we not discussed this before?"

"I want Superintendent Yeo to hear it from you."

"Does it interest him?"

"It might. Did you know that Ewen and Miss Wren had some sort of attachment?"

"It was rumoured."

"Miss Wren told me that when you and she were together, Ewen in his dressing-gown slipped in and a few minutes later your husband arrived. Can you explain that?"

"Then there were four of us," Sandra retorted. "Surely that was innocent enough? Ought we to have invited you?"

"It is not for me to say. Were you expecting either or both of them?"

"Why did you not join us and make it five?" she mocked.

"This is serious, Sandra. Were you expecting them?"

"I was not," she said after a moment's hesitation.

"All right. Let us accept that for the moment. You will remember I had met you and your husband that afternoon coming from the hut when I was on my way to the river. Had you by any chance noticed a green tartan scarf there then?"

"I had. I sat on it."

"It was not there the next day when I came to you meet you in rather odd circumstances."

"It was not. Had it been there I should not have wanted your help."

That so far supported what Jeremy and Rhoda had told. It was not only important in itself; it led to a more serious point in the story.

"Now, Sandra, I want you to consider this next question very carefully. The owner of the scarf and a friend knew they had left it behind and came back for it. They did not enter because they heard you and your husband quarrelling and they waited for you to go. Speaking of Ewen, you said 'I refuse to go through with it. It is caddish,' and later. 'If I do I shall stick to him.' Your husband said 'If you do I will shoot him.' Is that true?"

101

"Who were they?" she asked.

"That for the moment does not matter. I saw them there and they left just before you and your husband came out and met me."

Sandra's somewhat flippant manner deserted her. She could not fail to remember the words and she realised the gravity of the implication. To deny them would not be much good. She took time before she replied.

"Are you trying to make out that Ossie shot Ewen? If so you are utterly wrong."

"I am not trying to make out anything. I am asking simple questions to which you can reply or not as you see fit."

She looked at him, then at Yeo, and the others. It was some time before she spoke.

"All right," she said at last, "I am leaving Ossie anyhow. As you know so much you shall have the whole stinking story."

She paused, perhaps considering how she should put it.

"Ossie was broke. We both were. He knew Ewen liked me and he suggested if he could catch us in compromising circumstances he or his parents would pay heavily to hush things up. I did not like the idea but he persuaded me it was the only way to avoid a smash. Then Ewen invited us here for the week. That was to be the opportunity and was why we did not share a room."

No one spoke. After a few moments she went on:

"I liked Ewen. You may think I vamped him. He had always shown he thought a lot of me, but till then I had never taken him seriously. When I did he responded readily enough. On Thursday, the night before thee crowd came, he asked if he might come to my room, just to kiss me goodnight. I knew what it might mean and refused. When he pressed me I said 'Tomorrow perhaps.'

"Then I thought it over. I liked him and I felt I could not play him a dirty trick like that. I do not claim to be abnormally virtuous, but there are limits. On Friday afternoon I told Ossie I could not go on with it. We were in that hut. He was furious. He said everything was going well and I must not let him down."

"Excuse me a moment," Roger said, as she again paused, "was the idea that Ossie should divorce you and claim heavy damages?"

"I do not know," was the bitter reply. "He vowed it was not. There

102

was to be nothing really wrong; he was to claim for alienation of affection. The case was never to come into court. I had only to play a part. I said if Ewen wanted me I should stick to him. Ossie vowed he would shoot him if I did. Then we saw you and we left the hut. On the way to the house we argued again and I could see it was the damages he wanted; he didn't really care about me. I refused to be sold in whole or in part! I was done with him."

"Then that night?" Roger queried.

She laughed a little hysterically.

"That was comedy, unrehearsed comedy. I had not been able to tell Ewen he must not come. He was so busy the next day receiving his guests and preparing his speech. At bedtime I got Gwennie Wren to my room in case Ewen came. I think she stayed for the same reason! He did come. He was sick at finding Gwen there and did not know what to say. Then Ossie pushed in, hoping to find me and Ewen alone, but Gwen was there, too. I got rid of them all as soon as I could and that ended it."

"Have you a gun of any sort, Mrs. Henshaw?" Yeo broke in.

"I have not."

"Has your husband?"

"I believe he has."

"Is this it?" Yeo dramatically uncovered the weapon Gwennie Wren had brought to Roger. Sandra looked at it.

"It might be, but I think Ossie's is rather larger."

"Last night Ewen was shot, probably with this gun. Now can you recognise it?"

"You fool, you bloody fool!" Sandra exclaimed excitedly. "Have I told you all this and you cannot see that Ossie was the one person who wished to keep Ewen alive?"

"The language will not help you," Yeo said calmly. "I do not at all see that what you have admitted shows that your husband did not do what you tell us he threatened to do. He is the only person who to our absolute knowledge went into the garden that night."

"What can I to make you see sense? Ossie still hoped to persuade me. to agree to his plan. He had until next Wednesday to do so. Friday night would only have been a curtain raiser. The next act never happened because someone killed Ewen. I do not know who it was, but it was not Ossie!"

"You still love your husband," Yeo said. "You would like to save him?"

"Are you mad?" she returned stormily. "I had little reason to love him. He had squandered my money as well as his own. But I would save him from a charge of something he did not do. Would he shoot the golden goose before it laid a single egg? You told me those people heard me say I was done with it. I was. Why else did I have Gwen in my room? You believe me, Major Bennion?"

"Everything I know confirms your story, Sandra," he replied, "and I believe you believe it. Have you anything to say about the trick Gwen played on you the next afternoon?"

"It was just spite. Ewen did come to my room. She did not know I was done with him and with Ossie, too. She wanted to make a fool of me."

Then the door opened and Rhoda looked in.

"Excuse me if I am interrupting," she said. "We are just serving lunch. Will you join us or would you like something here?"

"Something here, if it is not troubling you," Yeo replied. "We have a lot to think about."

"No trouble," Rhoda said. "Some of the people are asking when they can go."

"No one is to go," he returned sharply. "We may want to see you again, Mrs. Henshaw."

The two young women left the room together, Sandra making no comment.

"Some glamour girl, that Sandra Henshaw," Yeo remarked. Her outburst had not affected him. He was too used to such things.

"Depends what you mean by glamour," Roger said.

"Got up to kill, though I am not charging her with that. Not yet any way."

"It is rather an insult to be called a glamour girl, though many people do not know it. It means illusory or false; something to deceive the eye, like a conjuring trick or a mirage. So far as Sandra is concerned her beauty is real."

104

"Which makes her more dangerous," Yeo commented. "It is of course possible her husband acted without her knowledge."

15

A Scrap of Paper

They were not meant to starve. One of the menservants brought in a large dish with cold chicken and sliced ham and tongue. Another brought a game pie and a bowl of salad. There was also a case of a dozen bottles of beer. Seeing that provision had been made for thirty guests who were not to come there was ample food in the house.

"Stewed peaches and cream to follow," Rhoda said. "Shall they be brought in now or later?"

"Now, I think," Roger replied, "and we shall not have to bother you again."

"That's all right. Ring if you want anything more."

"You are very good, my dear," Yeo said in a fatherly way. "Remember we are here to work."

Plates and cutlery were soon arranged and Rhoda left them to it. She had much else to attend to, not the least being to deal with telephone enquiries that poured in from many quarters as a result of her telegrams and messages of the night before. As she quitted the room Inspector Bellairs entered, led no doubt by professional instinct. A place was made for him.

"I have something, sir, I think you will want," he said to the superintendent. "The doctor extracted the bullets. Three of them. One in the head, two near the heart. Here they are." He handed over the three leaden objects carefully wrapped in soft paper.

"See if they fit the gun, Allenby," Yeo bade his assistant.

"You have the gun?" Bellairs asked in surprise.

"We have a gun," Yeo replied. "Whether it is the one we want remains to be seen."

"They are identical with those still here," Allenby reported. "Too big for the rook rifle."

"Then it will be up to ballistics to say if that gun fired them."

"Whose gun is it?" Bellairs enquired, astonished at the progress made in his absence.

"That we have still to discover," Yeo said.

They then gave undivided attention to the food placed before them. It dwindled with remarkable rapidity. The beer was also appreciated. Roger found the game pie to his liking; it had a crisp crust, unlike the soggy mess that so often serves as such, and the contents were not only kidney, bits of steak and unidentifiable bones. He was also busy with his thoughts and left the experts to do the talking.

"I spoke to the man outside," Bellairs remarked, after a time. "No finger-prints on the window. No clues anywhere. Too much rain for footmarks."

"No finger-prints on the gun," Sergeant Carston said, "except what may be Miss Wren's." He had attended to that. "I have to get hers."

"People are too wise to leave prints," Yeo muttered. "We have to thank the detective stories for that. Our only positive clue is the scrap of paper Major Bennion unearthed."

"What was that?" Bellairs asked.

Roger told him, completing the quotation.

"As he was ambitious I slew him," Bellairs repeated. "One of his political rivals?"

"Could be Roger said. "Or meant to look like it.'

The peaches and cream disappeared. The superintendent pushed back his chair, unfastened a waistcoat button and produced his pipe.

"Smoke if you like," he said. They all liked. When their pipes and cigarettes were going, he went on—"Let us consider how far we have got. You make a note, Carston, of the names and the chief points."

His sergeant produced a notebook and Biro pen and waited. "First I think we must put the Henshaws. She admits her husband threatened to shoot Ewen Jones, but I would not put it past her to do it herself and plant it on him, as she and Henshaw had quarrelled."

"Henshaw," Bellairs said. "The man I caught coming in from the garden, soaking wet."

Roger smiled faintly. The local man of course wanted all the credit he could get. It was not much.

"Had you searched him," Yeo said severely, "and not let him go upstairs to plant the gun in someone else's room it might have clinched the matter."

Bellairs made no answer. Roger remarked: "I do not think you can make a case against Mrs. Henshaw."

"We will consider that later," Yeo said. "She hates Gwennie Wren and could have put the gun in her room. Gwen says she found it among her clothes and she took it to Major Bennion. That is no proof she had not used it. She was breaking with Ewen or he had thrown her over. We have yet to see her, but she is certainly on the list."

That was duly noted and Allenby, following his hunch, said, "I think, sir, we should not overlook Jeremy Valiance who was alone in the garden when the crime was committed. Also of course there are Floss and Luke Catling."

"Put them down," Yeo nodded, "but barring the political angle, which we have not yet dealt with, I think it is a love affair. The eternal triangle—only it has four sides! The Henshaws, Gwennie Wren and Ewen. I will ask Lady Bethesda what she knows of Ewen's life with Gwen. Ring the bell and get these things cleared."

This was done and the men straightened their waistcoats. When the waiters appeared Rhoda also came to the door and beckoned to Roger.

"Can you spare a minute?" she asked.

"Of course," and he followed her to her room next door.

"Any news?" She spoke eagerly.

"Not of importance. They are jotting down possibilities many of which will cancel out when they seriously consider them."

"They do not seriously suspect Jeremy, as that man hinted?"

"His name is on their list, but that does not mean anything."

"It is too absurd," Rhoda said almost fiercely. "Apart from anything else what good could Ewen's death possibly do Jeremy?"

"At the moment," Roger replied, "they are considering Ewen's lady-loves. Had he any down here?"

"Not unless he brought them with him. He was here so seldom. I doubt if he spoke to a local girl except—" Then she stopped.

"Except," he repeated, "Angela Catling?"

"No. I know nothing of her more than Jeremy told you."

"Then except what?"

"Except nothing. I am an idiot. I do not want to give them another crazy idea."

"Better tell me."

"Jeremy has a sister Anna. A very pretty girl; she teaches, too, and keeps house for him. I introduced Ewen to her and they may have met two or three times. Your brainy brutes might say Ewen jilted her or something and so Jerry shot him for revenge! How do these boneheads get into the Force?"

Roger laughed. "I do not think the boneheads will accuse Jeremy or Anna unless they have much more to go on. Was that what you wanted to see me about?"

"Not at all." Rhoda laughed, too, a little ruefully. "It only shows how a silly word can start things when you are all on edge. I found something I thought might help you."

"What is it?"

"The letter from which that scrap of paper with the Brutus message was torn. This is it."

She took from her desk a sheet from which its companion half was missing. It was a brief typewritten letter dated from a Ladies' Club in London. It said:

Dear Lady Bethesda,

Thank you so much for the kind message Ewen gave me inviting me to spend the next week-end with you. I shall love to come. I hope you and Lord Bethesda and dear little Ambrose are well.

Yours very sincerely,

Gwennie Wren.

"Is that her usual address?" Roger asked.

"The only one I have. I believe it is a haunt of literary women."

"What makes you think the Brutus bit came from it?"

"She uses this sort of paper in her work. Folded double it serves for short letters. We have had others like it."

"The typing is certainly different."

"Yes. This was done on her own machine."

"You kept it on your desk?"

"Yes. I have a clip holding all the papers concerning a special event. When it is over I destroy them."

"Very methodical of you. You say many people came in here, so anyone wanting a bit of paper different from what they ordinarily use could have taken it and then typed the few words on your machine?"

"That is what I thought. I remembered it because of all the people asked Gwen was the only one to write to thank Lady Bethesda."

"A hit at me," Roger smiled. "I was guilty of that omission too. It did occur to me but I had never met her and Ewen assured me it was all in his hands. He said I might not see her."

"Will it help?"

"It helps to establish what our experts call an inside job and it may help to exonerate Gwen. She has plenty of paper and would not need to rifle your file for a bit of her own. But we must make sure of our facts. I will soon see if this fits with the bit we have."

16

It Never Happened!

Before returning to the room where Yeo and his assistants were at work Roger crossed the hall to see how the rest of the party were faring. The scene was peculiar.

The table had not been cleared. Their viands were similar to those the police had enjoyed, perhaps in greater profusion. There were wines as well as beer. Oswald Henshaw was the only person still at the table. He was in the act of refilling his glass from the port decanter. The M.P.s' ladies formed a group by themselves on seats near the window which had a view to the front of the house. Some of them were busy with the inevitable but praiseworthy knitting. Sandra, not far from them, had a book in her hand. Gwennie Wren had found a small desk and was busy scribbling. She might be sorry about Ewen but her professional instincts told her what a wonderful story it would make if she could be the first to get it to the Press.

The men clustered together round a fireplace at the end of the room. They were speaking very seriously but mostly in undertones. All talk stopped when Roger appeared.

"Can we go?" the burly Ruttle demanded.

"Not yet, I am afraid."

"Do they understand who we are?"

"Superintendent Yeo of Scotland Yard is in charge. He is dealing with everything as quickly as he can."

Roger spoke patiently. He knew Yeo would not be hustled in his handling of the case by the self-importance of the parties concerned.

"We are busy men in the public service," Ruttle said. "If there is any priority we should come first."

"He also is in the public service," Roger returned dryly.

"His duty lies here," Gibbons said. "We understand that. Ours does not. Surely he should let us get about our business?"

Then Sergeant Carston appeared at the door.

"Miss Wren, please."

Gwen got up, taking her note-book with her. Roger followed her out. Yet he would have been interested had he heard what those men were discussing.

Ewen Jones was to them no longer the possible leader of the day before, or the jolly good fellow of the previous night. He was dead and they were blaming him for the mess in which they found themselves. When the news of the gathering became known what would the Leaders of the Party say about it? What would be their attitude to the members of the Ginger Group? What would the

Unions think of the idea of the Supreme Council? Would Ewen's companions be regarded as rebels?

"I can at least say I was against him," Ruttle declared.

"Were you?" Edmonds asked. "I thought you proposed his toast."

"We were guests," Doodell said. "We had to be polite."

"Politeness did not call for the abolition of the Monarchy and all the rest of it," Boyne commented. "I wish I had never come."

They wrangled for some time. Then Gibbons, with his quiet smile, spoke.

"You are all making a great mistake. It never happened. There were no speeches. We chatted on various subjects but we were all waiting for the fellows who were to come today. That is the simpler line. It never happened. Surely we can keep our mouths shut."

"What about the women?" Doodell asked.

"Can we not keep them quiet?" Gibbons replied.

"But there will be a coroner's inquest," said Boyne. "Of course there will, but they cannot question everybody. We all tell the same story, the simpler the better."

"Who will keep Lady Bethesda quiet?" Ruttle demanded. "She hates us and will make mischief if she can."

"She will not attend the Party enquiry, if there is one," Gibbons said. "What do you think about it, Tom?"

This was to "Jeremiah" who had been listening but not speaking.

"Me? I do not remember much of what Ewen did say. I was waiting for him to come to what really concerns me. Moral up-lift. The degeneracy of much of the popular Press is what I want to see tackled. The space that is not devoted to semi-nude pictures is mostly given to some form of gambling. The papers themselves are little more than lottery tickets. They show rows of hats or blouses or coats and ask you to guess their order of merit in the opinion of the judges. Every guess costs three halfpence or perhaps sixpence. The prize may be a motor-car or a lump sum in cash or even a racehorse. It must pay well or they would not keep on doing it. They entice their readers to become gamblers."

Ruttle frowned at Gibbons. Why had he started "Jeremiah" on his pet theme?

"You are right, Tom," Gibbons said blandly. "Stick to that and it will be O.K."

It was at this point that Roger appeared. He then went with Gwennie Wren to the room where Yeo was sitting. Nothing of importance had transpired in his absence. Theories had been discussed but little progress made. Lady Bethesda had promised to come as soon as Master Ambrose and his nurse were ready to go out. So Gwen had been sent for.

Roger asked Yeo for the scrap of paper with the sinister Brutus message. When it was produced there was no doubt it had once been part of Gwen's letter. The rain had affected it, but the edges, including two slightly jagged tears, coincided.

"This was your letter to Lady Bethesda?" Yeo asked showing her the front portion.

"Part of it," Gwen replied. "I did not use a torn sheet."

"What about this?" He showed the portion found in the flower-bed.

"It looks like the other half. I did not type that on it. It was done by a different machine."

"Not by you?"

"Certainly not."

"It was found in the garden near the spot where the person who shot Ewen probably stood. Would you draw any conclusion from that?"

Gwen was silent for a moment or two.

"I might draw several," she said, "and they might all be wrong. I am not concerned in what happens to a scrap of my letter."

Yeo left it at that. It was fairly obvious she would not have used something so easily traceable to herself.

"I want you to let my assistant take your finger-prints to see if they tally with those on the weapon you took to Major Bennion, and if there are any others."

"I believe I could refuse," Gwen said, "but I won't." The simple operation was soon effected and she was given something on which to wipe her hands.

"Is that your permanent address?" Yeo pointed to the club heading on the letter.

"I have a room there."

"How often were you with Ewen Jones?"

A little colour showed on her cheeks, but she answered coolly enough. "Perhaps three times a week."

"You were closer to him than anyone else?"

"What exactly do you mean by that?" she returned, looking him straight in the face.

"I mean you were more in his confidence. Had he to your knowledge any enemy who might have wished him harm?"

"Not to the extent of murdering him!"

"You, if my information is correct, were angry with him for paying attention to another woman and you had the gun with which he was shot. Can you explain that?"

"I have explained it to Major Bennion. I was scared when I found it among my things and thought it best to take it to him. Should I have done that if I had used it? I was trying to help you. As to the other woman, if I was murderously inclined, and had I cared enough for him, I suppose I might have shot her. But I did not. Ewen and I were through."

"Do you know anything of a girl called Angela Catling?" Yeo asked abruptly.

"A little."

"A friend of Ewen Jones?"

Gwen smiled. "Definitely not."

"Her father tells us that Ewen enticed her to come to him in London. Is that true?"

"So the father shot him to avenge his innocent chee-ild? How did the father put the gun in my drawer?"

"I will ask the questions. Is the story true?"

"Most untrue." Gwen seemed amused.

"You mean to the best of your knowledge?" Yeo spoke sharply, a little annoyed at her manner.

"I mean to the best of my knowledge, but, as it happens, I know all there is to know."

"You had better tell me."

"Perhaps I had," Gwen laughed, "unless chasing red herrings is your favourite sport."

"Well?"

"I was here with Ewen about two months ago and we went to a show at the village hall. The girl Angela did a dance. Quite good for such a show and Ewen congratulated her afterwards. He said she ought to get a job in London. She said that was what she hoped to do. He told her if she did she should let him know, he might be able to help her."

"He gave her his address?"

"He did."

"That is what her father said."

"I thought you used the word enticed."

"Is not that what it amounted to? A few days later she left her home to go to him."

"She needed no enticing; she was jumping at a chance. A brassy sort of girl, probably thought she had only to be as near nude as possible to be a success. If Ewen had a fault, and I won't say he had not, he was a bit impulsive in offering to help people. He never expected to see her again. But one morning he got a letter from her saying she was arriving at Paddington that afternoon. He tossed it across to me. 'You had better meet her,' he said, 'you told her you might help her.' That was like him, too, though I believe I had said something of the sort."

"You met her?"

"I did. Ewen never saw her again and never knew what happened to her."

"What did happen?"

"Is that important?"

"It may be," Yeo said.

"Among my friends is Madame Zatta. You may have heard of her. She trains dancers and has troupes in many touring companies. I rang her up and asked if the girl would have a chance. She told me one of the 'Six Fairy Belles' appearing at Hastings had fallen and broken her leg. She had no one to take her place; was Angela any good? I said I thought she might pass. She begged me to bring her along to her rooms off the Haymarket. I did, and after trying her with a few steps Madame Zatta took her by the next train to Hastings. Madame Zatta, by the way, is a highly respectable person. She gives her girls food and lodging with a qualified woman to look after them, and a salary according to their merits."

"Is this true?" Yeo asked.

"Oh, no," Gwen said sarcastically. "All made up on the spur of the moment. But Madame Zatta is on the telephone. You could check it with her."

"Why did not Angela communicate with her parents?"

"Why ask me? She may have thought they would want to share her wages. It is rather rough that one of the good things Ewen did, or helped to do, should be used to smear his name."

"We have to follow any line that is brought to us," Yeo said, "even if it is a dead end."

"If I may ask a question," Roger said, "what were you so busy on when I came into the dining-room just now?"

"I was writing down what I remember of Ewen's speech and what the others said about it, and my impressions generally."

"I thought it might be that. A useful record."

"I would like to see it," Yeo said.

She smiled. "My own brand of shorthand. Not much use to anyone else."

"We can deal with all brands," he returned. "Is that the book?"

"It is. I do not think it will help you."

"You shall have it back when we are satisfied about that." She was reluctantly handing it over when Rhoda reappeared to say that Lady Bethesda was at liberty if they wished to see her again. Yeo said he would be glad to do so, and told Gwen that was all for the present.

Lady Bethesda took the seat she had occupied before. Her manner was a little more haughty.

"You wish to see me again?" she said.

"I am wondering if you can tell me a little more about Ewen's private life?" Yeo replied.

"I do not think so. His duties kept him in town. We saw little of him."

"What of his week-ends and holidays?"

"He seldom spent them here."

"You told me he brought Miss Wren and Captain and Mrs. Henshaw on previous occasions. Any others—ladies perhaps?"

"No one who is here now. He did bring young women on two occasions. He called them actresses. His father and I did not approve of them."

"He was fond of ladies?"

Lady Bethesda pursed her lips and made no answer.

"I am told he was very attentive to Mrs. Henshaw. Is that so?"

"If it is, it was her husband's concern, not mine," was the prim reply.

"What were his exact relations with Miss Wren?"

"Others may tell you. I cannot."

"She admits that she and Ewen had lived together from time to time. Were you aware of that?"

"I was not," was the chilly reply, "but it does not entirely surprise me."

"There is really nothing you can tell me that will help to show who may have shot him?"

"I regret there is not. Lord Bethesda has been ill for some time. I was very anxious, but Ewen troubled little about us. I can however tell you that Dr. Strange has seen his lordship and is willing for him to come down, presently, perhaps in an hour's time when he has finished his rest and if it is really necessary. I do not think he can add to what I have told you."

"I could see him upstairs if that would be better."

"I will ask him."

She rose. So did Yeo, but he said, "One more question, please. I asked it before, but are you fully satisfied that no one could have left and re-entered the TV room during the performance?"

"I answered it before. I cannot say it is impossible. When you are absorbed in a play you may not notice all that goes on

116

around you in the dark but I was not aware of anything of the sort."

With that she left the room.

"Not much help there," Yeo muttered. "What do you say, Bennion?"

"You have not yet explored the political angle," Roger said. "Ruttle is getting impatient."

"He will keep. We will try to clear up this first. Do you believe Gwennie Wren's story?"

"I do, but you can easily phone Madame Zatta. You can also give her address to Luke Catling. A letter there to his Angela will no doubt reach her. As Gwen said he will probably expect some of her earnings."

"Not unlikely. Let's see Henshaw."

17

"Where is Your Gun?"

Captain Henshaw entered the room with something of a swagger. Perhaps as other soldiers have done he thought the best defence was to attack. Possibly the port had had an effect.

"Before you ask me questions," he said, "there are one or two I would like you to answer."

"What are they?" Yeo frowned.

"What was Gwennie Wren doing in Major Bennion's bedroom between twelve and one last night, or rather this morning? What did those M.P.s mean when I heard them mutter, 'It never happened. We must keep our mouths shut'?"

So, Roger thought, it was Henshaw's door he had heard closing when Gwen left him. But it was for Yeo to reply. This the superintendent did in his sternest manner.

117

"I cannot answer your second question but I will the first. Miss Wren had found in her bedroom the gun that probably shot Ewen Jones; put there, I have reason to think, by yourself. Why else were you spying on her?"

"I was not spying. I had been to the bathroom and I chanced to see her enter his room. I waited to see how long she would remain. As to my putting a gun in her room, that is absurd."

"Yet," Yeo said slowly, "you had threatened to shoot Ewen Jones?"

"That is a lie!"

"Is it? I will tell you the case against you, Captain Henshaw, as verified by witnesses. You can then give me an explanation if you care to do so. You can of course refuse, but I have proof for what I am going to say. You will understand that your reply will be taken down and may be used as evidence."

"Fire away," Ossie muttered, but the swagger had gone. He lit a cigarette. His hand was not too steady.

"Before you came here you urged your wife to encourage Ewen Jones to pay attentions to her. Your object in so doing was you could bring an action against him and claim heavy damages. To make this easy you asked for you and your wife to have separate rooms. On Friday afternoon you quarrelled with your wife in that hut by the river. She refused to be a party to the conspiracy. She said as you valued her so lightly if Ewen really wanted her she would go to him. You told her if she did you would shoot him."

Ossie was staring at Roger Bennion. He had seen him approaching the hut; it was impossible for him to have heard what was said.

"Quite untrue," he muttered.

"I have it not only on the evidence of your wife," Yeo said, "but two young people had left a scarf in the hut and came back for it. Perhaps you noticed it there. As they heard voices they waited for you to go. They also heard what you and your wife were saying to one another. Their story and hers tally."

Ossie tried to look unconcerned. "Who are these young people?" he asked.

"That you will know in due course," Yeo replied. "Later that night you followed Ewen to your wife's room hoping to catch them there together. They were together, but Miss Wren was with them. Your wife had brought her for protection. The next night Ewen was shot.

You did not join the party in the TV room but you had a game of billiards and then went into the garden. You were there when he was shot and so far as I can ascertain no one else left the house. You came in wet, and after a few words with Inspector Bellairs you said you must go upstairs to change your clothes. That gave you the opportunity to put the gun in Miss Wren's room. After that, as you have told me, you watched her to see what she would do if she found it. Have you anything to say?"

"Plenty," the captain replied, making an effort to master any fears he may have felt. "You say you got most of this from Sandra, my wife?"

"She made a statement which in material respects is confirmed."

"Sandra is a liar. I will not deny we had a tiff in the hut, but it was because she had been flirting with Ewen and I objected. Her story of a conspiracy is sheer invention; her word against mine. We had separate rooms because there was a shortage of married quarters. Rhoda will confirm that. As to my threatening to shoot Ewen, I do not admit it but one may talk a bit wildly when one finds one's wife carrying on with another man and reluctant to give him up. I played billiards with Major Bennion and then went into the garden and got caught in the rain, as I explained to him and the inspector. I did not shoot Ewen as, apart from anything else, I had not got a gun."

"Do you deny that this is your gun?" Yeo produced the weapon Gwen had handed to Roger.

Ossie glanced at it.

"Certainly I do. I have one rather like it, but mine is heavier and has my initials on it."

Roger whispered to the superintendent.

"Where is your gun?" the latter enquired.

"In my room in my hotel."

"Then if sent there we shall find it?"

Ossie hesitated. "Certainly, unless I have been robbed."

"Where exactly is it?"

"In a locked case in the bottom drawer of my dressing-chest."

"Perhaps Captain Henshaw, in your hearing, Superintendent," Roger suggested, "would telephone the manager of the hotel to give your representative access to it. It need not be said he comes from the Yard. You should get his report in less than an hour and that will clear up this point—unless of course Captain Henshaw has two guns, one without initials."

"What should I want with two guns?" Henshaw said angrily. "I do not like my things messed about in my absence, but I will do what you say if it will satisfy you."

"I could get a warrant." Yeo said, "but this may be quicker."

There was a telephone in the room and he got through at once to Scotland Yard and gave the necessary instructions. "You can just call yourself Walter Wingate," he added to the plain-clothes officer to whom he was speaking.

Henshaw then spoke to his hotel and gave the message Yeo dictated, saying Mr. Walter Wingate was on his way.

"I shall ask you to stay with one of my men until we get the reply," Yeo said. He did not know what other telephones there might be in the house and was taking no risks. "But first you might tell me what you meant by your other question. What was it the M.P.s said never happened and they must keep their mouths shut?"

"If I knew that I should not have asked you," Henshaw replied in a surly manner. "One of them said something about making Lady Bethesda hold her tongue."

"You do not know to what they were referring?"

"I was not listening. They were all nattering together, but occasionally one of them raised his voice."

Yeo frowned. "While you are waiting you might see if you can remember any more."

As the captain left the room Yeo turned to Roger. "What do you make of him?"

"A glib liar," was the reply. "His first line also was, it never happened, but he owned to a good deal when he realised how much 'we knew. Whether he had urged Sandra to flirt with Ewen or was remonstrating with her for so doing is difficult to prove. I would sooner believe her story than his, and what Jeremy Valiance told us supports it. A wife cannot or need not give evidence against her husband, but it is the gun that matters. There she supported him, saying this was not his and his was bigger. If his is found where he says, it pretty well lets him out, unless you can prove he also had the use of another."

"What of his tale about the M.P.s?"

"It might be true or he might be trying to raise fresh suspicions. You must get it from them."

"I will. I'll start on that fellow Ruttle."

But there was a digression. Rhoda came in to tell them Mr. Barclay Willis, the vicar of the parish, had called to express his sympathy with Lord and Lady Bethesda. Lady Bethesda had said they were not at home to anyone. Would they care to see him or should she just take his message?

"He might be able to give us a little local colour," Yeo said. "Ask him to come here."

The Reverend Barclay Willis was a tall, middle-aged man, no doubt very worthy and anxious to do his duty by his parishioners. He was not eloquent but his cure was his only care, beyond an insatiable fondness for crossword puzzles.

"I am a superintendent from Scotland Yard," Yeo said when he entered, handing him a card. "I am enquiring into the death of Ewen Jones. How did you hear of it?"

"Dear, dear. This is very distressing. I take it foul play is suspected. I heard of it from Mr. Valiance, our schoolmaster. I felt I must come to express my deep sympathy with the bereaved parents. It must be a terrible shock for them."

"Did you know their son personally?"

"Oh, yes, but not intimately. He was not often here."

"Did they attend your church?"

"Lord Bethesda did when his health permitted. Lady Bethesda is a very regular member of my congregation and a great helper in all good works. Mr. Ewen we saw but seldom. I tried to enlist his aid, but owing to an unfortunate incident he kept away."

"What was the unfortunate incident?" Yeo asked.

"Oh, trivial and quite irrelevant. It cannot help you at all."

"I would like to hear it."

"Well, it was years ago. I hoped to interest him in our lads' institute. He came once or twice, and then he agreed to captain our side in a cricket match against Little Beeford, an adjacent village. He kept wicket for us. I used to play at one time myself. I may be wrong as to the exact figures but I think the Little Beth, as our lads called them, were all out for 72. We made that exact number for nine wickets and Mr. Ewen had to go in. He modestly put himself last as he was a big man and the others only boys. It seemed a certain victory for us. He made what they called a mighty swipe at his first ball. He missed it and was bowled. It caused much laughter and has never been forgotten. They still talk of it. After that we saw very little of him. It was indeed most unfortunate, most unfortunate."

"Was he popular in the village?"

"He was respected, both as his father's son and as a Member of Parliament."

"Was there ever any village scandal in which he was concerned?"

"Oh no, certainly not. Or I would have been the first to hear of it."

Or the last, Yeo thought. "Was his name ever coupled with that of Angela Catling?"

"Not that I am aware of." Mr. Willis spoke more stiffly. "She was a restless sort of girl and went away to learn dancing or acting."

"You know her parents?"

"Certainly I do."

"Did they say Mr. Ewen was responsible for her going away?"

"Oh dear, no. Never."

"Her father suggested it to me," Yeo said.

'That must be wrong, quite wrong. Catling is not a very reliable person."

"Is there anyone else who, so far as you know, had reason to wish ill for Mr. Ewen?"

"I am sure not," the vicar replied. "Quite sure."

"He was murdered," Yeo said gravely. "He was here with a party of friends. It would appear that either one of those friends murdered him or it was some local person. You think I can disregard the latter?"

"It is distressing, very distressing," the vicar said again, "but yes, I feel sure you can."

Then Roger Bennion put a question.

"Am I right, sir, in thinking the cricket match of which you told us was the last played on this ground?"

"Quite right. But you must not connect the two things. It was at that time little Ambrose was born. Lady Bethesda was naturally anxious for him and did not want to risk his getting infection of any kind. Our youngsters are clean and healthy but, of course, you get measles and whooping-cough and the like every where. She also feared he might pick up coarse expressions."

"A little early for that." Yeo commented. "Did the closing of the ground cause resentment?"

"Oh, no. It was at the end of the season and the next year Lord Bethesda saw that the village green was made fit for play and bought an old army hut for them to use as a pavilion. I think they preferred it."

"Was there not trouble over a right of way beside the river?" Roger asked.

"Years ago, but that was in Mr. Marden's time, before his daughter's marriage. When Lord Bethesda came he was very kind. He allowed the cricket here and then helped with the village green, as I said. The right of way trouble was forgotten."

"Was Jeremy Valiance here at the time of that trouble?" Yeo enquired.

"Oh no. Not till years later."

"What is your opinion of him?"

"An estimable young man in every way," the vicar replied. "A hard worker and a good influence with our young people. He gets on well too with the parents, not always an easy matter."

"He never had any difference with Mr. Ewen?"

"I feel sure not. They seldom met."

"What of Dan Floss and the rest of the staff here? I suppose you know them?"

"Oh, yes. I like to know all my parishioners, irrespective of their station. All very respectable people."

123

"Thank you, Mr. Willis. You cannot help us?"

"I regret deeply that I cannot. It is sad, most sad. I feel sorely upset. A gifted gentleman and so young. I assume there will be an inquest, though I am not conversant with such matters. Nothing of the sort has ever happened before in this neighbourhood, at least not in my time. Please assure his lordship and her ladyship of my most sincere sympathy. Should they desire the interment to take place here I will of course carry out their wishes in every respect. But I quite understand the shock is too sudden for them to consider such things yet."

When he had departed Yeo remarked, "That does not tell us much. Quite a model village! I did not expect him to say otherwise."

"To a psychiatrist," Roger commented, "the cricket incident might throw a light on Ewen's character. He could not bear to be laughed at as a failure. But that again does not help a lot."

"He was a failure all right, except with the ladies," Yeo said. "We had better tackle this Bill Ruttle."

18

Denials and Evasions

"I consider, Superintendent, you have shown us very little consideration. I know you are faced with a difficult and unpleasant task, but we also have important work to do."

This was Big Bill's utterance when he strode into the room and took a chair uninvited. Only Yeo, Roger and Allenby were there, the last named taking the necessary notes. Bellairs had been given a job and Carston was in charge of Captain Henshaw. They were in the billiards-room and Ossie was trying to use the time to win a few shillings at snooker. Carston was fairly adept at the game but resisted the temptation.

"I believe you came for the week-end, Mr. Ruttle. I hope to be able to let you go tomorrow," Yeo was saying.

"Tomorrow! You expect me to stay another night?"

"That may depend on the assistance you can give me," Yeo retorted calmly. "I have read the statement you made to Inspector Bellairs. Have you anything to add to it?"

"Nothing. That is why I object to being kept waiting in this manner."

"I understand you did not join the television party but came to this room to write your notes. You never left the house?"

"I have already said so."

"And you subsequently destroyed your notes?"

"I also said that."

"You saw no one and no one saw you until after the crime was committed and discovered?"

"As I was alone in this room that is obvious. I am a patient man but what is the object of this repetition? It is waste of time."

Yeo disregarded his anger. "Everyone in the party was supposed to be a friend of Ewen Jones?"

"A further discovery of the obvious!"

"Can you suggest any one of them who might for any reason have shot him?"

"Some of them are strangers to me. I can suggest nothing."

"You arrived on Friday. Were your discussions at dinner that night entirely amicable?"

Ruttle looked at Roger Bennion. He also had been present. Was his another mouth that would have to be shut?

"Politicians cannot always see eye to eye but they remain friends. Ewen made suggestions we could not all agree with. I think Major Bennion's criticisms were as hostile as any."

Roger smiled but made no comment. He apparently was to be the scapegoat for all of them.

"Would you say Ewen was ambitious?" Yeo proceeded.

"Most definitely I would. His every effort was to push himself forward."

"You would regard that as wrong?"

"Not necessarily. I suppose when you were a constable you were ambitious or you would not now be a superintendent."

"Can you use a typewriter?"

"Me? What is the idea?" He showed his big fingers. "I never tried. Expect I'd hit three letters at once. What are girls for?"

Yeo did not seem to think that line worth pursuing.

"I believe," he said, "while you and your fellow Members were together after lunch you discussed certain matters and agreed you must keep your mouths shut about them. Is it true?"

"Who the devil told you that?" Ruttle cried angrily. "Did you expect us to sit silent until it pleased you to see us?"

"I take it then it is true. You also said that something never happened. To what did that refer?"

"Have you been listening at the door?" This was Ruttle to Roger.

"I cannot help you this time," was the reply. "I had not been listening."

Had someone played traitor? Ruttle controlled his anger. The matter must be handled carefully.

"Since you say we agreed to keep our mouths shut," he said to Yeo, "this seems a good time to begin. I can however tell you it was nothing that concerns you. Purely a question of politics."

"Then why was it necessary that Lady Bethesda should also keep her mouth shut?"

Ruttle was disconcerted. For a moment he did not know what to reply. Was there some concealed phone in the room? How otherwise could their talk have been heard? It was odd perhaps that he had forgotten Captain Henshaw who had been some way off and was actually behind him.

"I cannot answer that. If it was said, it was in jest."

"You refuse to tell me what you were discussing?"

"I do. Members of Parliament have some rights and privileges, if even they are listened to and spied on."

"You disappoint me, Mr. Ruttle," Yeo said severely. "Being a Member of Parliament I looked for some co-operation from you when a fellow Member had been murdered. You have been obstructive rather than helpful. You might have been the murderer yourself since we have no evidence as to your movements at the time of the crime. You were making notes, but those notes have disappeared! I must ask you to remain in the house until I say you can go."

"This is infamous," Ruttle cried. "I shall lodge a complaint in the proper quarter. You will regret your insolence."

Yeo did not answer. He whispered to Inspector Allenby to find Mr. Gibbons and to see that the two M.P.s did not speak to one another. There was silence in the room until Gibbons appeared. Ruttle had risen to his feet and was standing with his hands thrust into the pockets of his tweed jacket. He was aware he had not shown to advantage but at least he had given nothing away.

"That is all for the present, Mr. Ruttle," Yeo said when his companion Member entered.

"And it is all I have to say, now or at any time," was the retort. But Big Bill departed with much less assurance than had entered. Roger had taken no part in the questioning; he thought it a matter for the police to handle and felt the superintendent had done it quite well.

There was no bluster about Fred Gibbons. He came in smiling and spoke in his usual suave manner.

"Glad to see you at last, Superintendent," he said. "This is a terrible affair. I wish I could help you, but I expect you know what I told the inspector last night. I am afraid there is nothing I can add to it. I shall miss poor Ewen very much. He was a splendid fellow."

"Your story is that after dinner that night you went to your bedroom to read and did not come down until after the crime had been discovered?"

"That is so. I tried first to get a four for bridge but no one seemed keen to play. I had an interesting detective story and decided to finish it. When I had done so I went to join the others, horrified at what they told me. Poor, poor Ewen. I have lost a very valued friend."

"You realise, Mr. Gibbons, that with the exception of Mr. Ruttle and perhaps Captain Henshaw you are the only member of the party who has no alibi for the time of the crime?"

"I am not aware of that. Naturally I did not know what anyone else was doing. I can only tell you how I myself was occupied. As to alibis, I find in the books I read the guilty person is generally the one with the best alibi."

"That is not my experience," Yeo commented dryly. "I gather you

127

are interested in crime and have some knowledge of the ways of criminals?"

"That is not quite fair," Gibbons laughed. "If you were to suspect everybody who read detective stories, few would escape suspicion. It is just a matter of pitting your wits against those of the author."

"That may be so. There is something else that interests me. I am informed that after lunch you and your friends were discussing why you must keep your mouths shut. Will you elaborate?"

"So Bill Ruttle has been blabbing," Gibbons said, evidently annoyed. "Is not what he told you enough?'

"From your knowledge of your choice of fiction you must be aware that the police always require confirmation of what they hear. I would like your version of it."

Gibbons considered this for some moments. Roger Bennion was amused at Yeo's adroitness.

"It had nothing to do with Ewen's death, though that in a way was the cause of it. Our meeting here was to be kept a secret until we decided on our plan of action. Ewen's death made that impossible. We were sheep without a shepherd. The story of the meeting is bound to become known and the Party chiefs are almost sure to ask what it was all about. Ewen took a line that might well have caused a party split, so I suggested as the big meeting had not taken place and nothing had been agreed we should disregard what he had said as though it had never been uttered. My idea was to avoid trouble. I hope Ruttle told you so."

"Why was Lady Bethesda's mouth to be shut?" Yeo enquired.

"What did Ruttle say about that?"

"I am asking what you say about it," Yeo retorted.

"I am surprised Bill Ruttle mentioned it," Gibbons said, with rather a forced smile. "I forget who it was, but someone thought my plans would not work as Lady Bethesda did not approve of us and might try to make difficulties. That is all there was to it. We reached no decision."

"Had you all agreed with Ewen's proposals?"

"Indeed, no. I for one had not."

"You regarded him as ambitious?" Yeo put his inevitable question.

"I suppose, in a way, we did. If you start a movement you no doubt expect to play a prominent part in it."

"You were against him?"

"In some respects. Not all."

"Were any of you against him sufficiently to make his removal desirable?"

"Certainly not," Gibbons replied warmly. "We do not take our politics like that in this country. If we did several members of both parties might be removed. I think, Superintendent, if I may say so, you are barking up the wrong tree. Poor Ewen's death had nothing to do with politics."

"What else can you suggest?"

"I hate to speak ill of a friend, but I would like to avenge him. That Ewen and Gwennie Wren had lived together is common knowledge, though we did not talk about it. It was not our affair. But down here they openly quarrelled and Ewen deserted her for Sandra Henshaw, despite her husband's presence. I accuse nobody, but I think that is the line for you to investigate."

"Can you tell me anything to support it?"

"Nothing very definite. Sandra and her husband ignored one another. Why were they here? Neither of them knew the first word about politics. They both told us so. Then Gwen, who does, found herself neglected for the other woman. It is a complicated situation, but I think, Superintendent, a man of your experience and ability, especially aided by Major Bennion, will surely find the right solution."

"Very handsome of you, Mr. Gibbons," Roger said. "You may have helped us more than you think. What, by the way, was the title of the book you were reading and who was the villain?"

"I will get it for you if you like," Gibbons offered.

"Don't trouble to do that. Tell me the names and I will know if I have read it."

"No trouble at all. I am not good at remembering names. 'Sleeping Death' or something like that."

"And the villain?"

"I an not quite sure. It is rather poor stuff and I went to sleep over it."

"That is not what you told us before," Yeo said sharply, "nor what you told Inspector Bellairs. You admitted you had been in the garden and your shoes were dirty!"

"Really, Superintendent," Gibbons said, with some show of indignation, "I hope you are not suggesting I had anything to do with the death of my friend. I did not mention I had fallen asleep, it seemed so immaterial, due to a late night and a busy day. I did say I had been in the porch or just beyond it looking for bridge players, and I never clean my shoes myself."

"There is nothing else you wish to tell me, or to explain?" Yeo asked grimly.

"Nothing. I am sorry my efforts to assist you are not appreciated."

"But you admit your statement that you went to your room to finish your story is not true?"

"I admit nothing of the sort," Gibbons said in his more soothing manner. "Cannot you see, my dear fellow, I went to my room for that purpose, but I fell asleep."

"For which there is no confirmation?"

"How could there be? When I came down I knew nothing of what had happened. Everyone can confirm that."

"Or can confirm that you said so," Yeo commented dryly. "That is all for the present. I may want to see you again."

"There is something else I can tell you," Gibbons said suddenly. "There may be nothing in it, but perhaps you have not had time to investigate it."

"What is it?"

"As you may be aware this is a very old house. I have been making enquiries and looking about a bit. Below this floor there is a labyrinth of disused rooms. Any enemy of Ewen's could easily hide there. He might be there now! There are vast possibilities you should not overlook. There might even be a secret passage into the grounds."

"Thank you," Yeo aid dryly. "I can see your study of mystery stories has not been entirely wasted."

19

His Lordship

"A pretty trio," Yeo muttered. "Henshaw, Ruttle and Gibbons. All of 'em twisting the truth and any of 'em could have done it. Which was it?"

"The one that had the gun—if you can prove it," Roger replied. "I would not trust Gibbons. Ewen was his dear friend but he was quick to give the story of him and Gwennie Wren. Yet I do not see him as a murderer."

"Why not?"

"Intrigue and treachery would be his weapons. From what we know of their keep-your-mouths-shut talk I can imagine him going to the Party chiefs to sell his fellow rebels if there was trouble. He might have sold Ewen, too, had his plans taken shape—of course from the highest motives. But I cannot see why he should kill him just at that moment. He would have waited for the bigger meeting to see how the cat jumped."

"What put you on to his lie about the book?" Yeo asked.

"A chance shot. A man's reading may influence his actions. He was rather vague about it and you generally have to get to the last chapter to know who-dun-it. Also I could not why a guest who wanted to finish a book should go to his rather poky bedroom to do it when there are lounges where he could be so much more comfortable."

"It was all a lie?"

"He may have been tired and wanted a nap."

"Hm. What do you think of his man in the basement idea?"

"Not much. It is true there are disused rooms there and failing everything else they could be searched, but I doubt if anyone using them could have known about the television room and its arrangements."

Then the ever-useful Rhoda came in to say that Lord Bethesda was in her room and would see them as soon as they were ready.

"Bring him in now," Yeo said.

"He seems really ill," the girl ventured. "I hope you will not keep him long. He ought to go back to bed."

She disappeared and returned a few moments later, supporting her uncle on her arm. He walked slowly, and certainly seemed more infirm than he had been two days before. Even his hair was whiter. He was fully dressed, having a dark suit and a black tie. The men stood until Rhoda with Roger's aid had him seated in the most comfortable chair.

"I am sorry we have to trouble you, my lord," Yeo began, "and I hope you will allow me to express our sympathy in the shock you have sustained. I can assure you we will do our utmost to bring the guilty party to justice."

Lord Bethesda murmured words of thanks in a shaky voice.

"I believe the gathering here on Friday was of your son's friends rather than yours?"

A nod gave assent.

"But you knew them?"

"Not all of them."

"Can you tell me which?"

"I knew Bill Ruttle and Fred Gibbons and old Dayton, Jeremiah as they called him. I think I once met Boyne. The rest I only knew by name. A later generation than mine."

"You are referring of course to the M.P.s and their wives?"

"Yes. I do not think I had met the wives."

"Would you think it possible that one of his fellow Members could have killed your son?"

The old man was silent for some moments. Then he shook his head. "I should think it quite impossible."

"The others in the party," Yeo proceeded, "apart from Major Bennion, were Miss Wren and Captain and Mrs. Henshaw. You knew them?"

"They have been here before."

"Could one of them have had a hostile feeling towards Mr. Ewen?"

Lord Bethesda raised a thin white hand to his forehead and stroked back his hair. "I know of none," he said wearily.

"Why were they here?"

"Miss Wren is a writer and has influence in political circles. She had worked with Ewen for some time. The Henshaws were his personal friends, paying a longer visit."

"I have reason to believe that Captain Henshaw is financially in very low water. Could he have been hoping to get money from your son?"

"Most unlikely. He and my son were fellow officers and he must have known Ewen could not help him."

Yeo decided that until he had the report as to Henshaw's gun it would be better not to pursue that line further.

"You must pardon me if I seem persistent," he said, "and I know how distressing it is to you, but from our enquiries it seems that the crime must be attributed to one of the persons we have alluded to. Will you tell me the precise object of their meeting here?"

"My son considered our Party was lacking in push. He wished to form an action group to stimulate them. A Ginger Group, he called it."

"I believe on the day they arrived, on the Friday evening, you asked him to outline his proposals?"

"That is so."

"Were you previously aware of them?"

Again the stroke of the forehead. "I was not."

"They were very advanced, almost revolutionary in character."

"In some respects, yes."

"Is it possible they went far enough to provoke active hostility?"

A shake of the head. "I should not think so. Hot-headed young men get wild ideas and love notoriety. They learn better as they grow older. They provoke opposition but not—murder."

He whispered the last word, but otherwise was speaking more firmly.

"Lord Bethesda, was your son a Communist?"

After a pause the reply came—"Yes and no."

"Will you please tell me what you mean by that?" Yeo spoke quietly, but he did not mean to be put off.

"Most of our Socialists are Communists, though many of them are not aware of the fact. The two words mean practically the same thing: the ownership and control of means of production, of capital and land, and their administration in the interests of all. But our Socialists are not prepared to take orders from Moscow. The Russians have been ruled by tyrants for centuries and to change a Tsar for a Lenin or a Stalin seemed good to them and to some extent improved their condition. We are far in advance of that and believe in government by the people. The British would never accept government by a dictator or a group of dictators."

His tone was emphatic and for once there seemed almost a gleam of the old Welsh Lion.

"Did not your son suggest something of the sort, though I believe he called it a Grand Council of Trade Unions?"

"He did, but it was not to supersede Parliament. It might have led to a clash."

"Thank you, my lord. I think I understand." Yeo said it, but whether he did or not would be hard to say. "May I turn to another matter, your son's private life. Can you tell me anything of that?

"In what way? Are you referring to the fact that he lived in a sort of almshouse?"

"Not exactly. Rather to the fact that he did not live there alone."

"What do you mean?"

"I do not wish to pain you, but the fact may have to come out. He lived there with his mistress, Gwennie Wren."

This obviously shook the old man. His head sunk forward a little. He looked at Roger. "You did not tell me this. Is it true?"

"I am afraid it is," Roger replied.

"I do not suggest it accounts for his death," Yeo said. "Miss Wren admits their association but asserts there has been a coolness between them. She has almost, if not entirely, convinced me of her innocence of the crime. I am anxious to know if your son had entanglements with any other woman?"

It took Lord Bethesda some moments to recover control of his emotions.

"I know nothing of his association with Miss Wren nor of anything else of the sort. Perhaps I was to blame for not interesting myself

134

more in his life. Things here were quiet for him. He seemed so occupied with his work. No breath of scandal ever reached me."

"Thank you, my lord. I regret having had to mention it but I do not think it can be concealed. There is one other matter I might mention. We have been told there are a number of disused rooms in your basement quarters and it would be possible for an enemy to hide there and then to commit the crime. Can you say anything about that?"

A faint smile flickered on the old man's face.

"I should say it is quite impossible. There are rooms down there and in the past some antiquarian societies asked to see them. They found little to interest them. It has all been closed for several years."

"The little-ease?" Roger queried.

"The rooms were mostly store-rooms but one or two were found that it was suggested had been punishment or penitential cells. It was not definitely established."

"But is there access to or from them now?" Yeo asked.

"There is not. They were approached by narrow stairs from the old kitchen. That approach is now boarded over and nailed down. It is also covered with linoleum. No access is possible."

"Thank you," Yeo said. "We have no evidence to support any such suggestion, but as it was mentioned I thought we ought to dispose of it. I do not know if there is anything Major Bennion would like to ask you."

"Not on that point," Roger replied, "but I might perhaps say it was whispered among the dwellers in my father's cottages that Miss Wren lived there with your son and that was one of the reasons for our wishing him to go. I did not mention it before and I do not think it need become public now."

"I hope not," Bethesda murmured. "No one told me."

"I can understand that," Roger said sympathetically. "There are two other matters, quite different, I would like to be clear about. I am not well versed in Trade Union procedure but I believe there are certain appointments to which a promising member may aspire. He may become a District Secretary or a Regional Organiser. Then he may be elected to the National Executive which has possibilities of the highest Cabinet rank. I have been told there is likely to be a vacancy shortly in the National Executive and that Ruttle, Gibbons and your son may have aspired to fill it. Could that have created a serious rivalry between them?"

"My son never filled any of the minor posts," Bethesda replied in a slow, deliberate manner. "He may have thought his Ginger Group would be a short cut to the National Executive. He never said so and I do not think it would have served his purpose. I cannot speak in any way for Ruttle or Gibbons."

"They, or either of them, might have regarded Ewen as a danger to their prospects?"

"I cannot say."

"Thank you," Roger said. He then reached across the table and took the chart he had originally made of the seats occupied by the parties attending the TV show on the night of the tragedy.

"The other point is more a matter of fact or routine. You will remember I made this sketch after the crime was discovered and before the police took over. You agreed it was correct?"

"I did."

"You occupied the seat number 23, nearest to the door. You would therefore be in the best position for knowing if anyone left the room, or re-entered it, during the show."

"That would be so."

"You are convinced that in fact no one did?"

His lordship hesitated. "Convinced is a strong word. My attention was riveted on the picture."

"You were aware when Lady Bethesda turned on the light?"

"We all were."

"She brushed past you, she did not ask you to do it?"

"I hardly remember. The scream a moment later—" Before he could finish the sentence there was another scream. A piercing scream very like the one on the fatal night. But it was not in that room. It came from outside or above. It was prolonged and was followed by hurrying footsteps.

There was a startled silence in the room for some moments.

"See what that is," Yeo said to Allenby.

The inspector rose but, before he could reach the door, it

opened and Sergeant Carston appeared. The screams grew louder.

"What is it?" Yeo asked.

"Lady Bethesda," the sergeant said in his stolid way. "You had better come, sir."

"What do you mean? Has she asked for me?"

"She couldn't. She is dead. She has been strangled."

20

The Second Tragedy

There was another moment of stunned silence. Then they all rose to their feet, all but Lord Bethesda. He tried to rise but sank back into his chair, Roger went to his side and helped him.

"Where?" Yeo was asking.

"Upstairs," Carston said.

They moved the door, Roger and his lordship being in the rear. They saw on the landing above them that the screams came from Brigid the nurse. Rhoda, her cheeks ashy pale, was holding her, trying to soothe her hysterical weeping. Little Ambrose was with them, not crying but staring with solemn startled eyes as though he could not understand it. Other doors were opened. Ossie Henshaw looked out of the billiards room and a group of the M.P.s and their wives emerged from the dining-room. Sandra and Gwennie Wren were there, too. The front door also was open as the constable on duty outside wished to see what was happening.

Yeo led the way, dashing up the stairs with amazing rapidity for a man of his age and build.

"Where is she?" he asked when he reached the little group on the landing.

Rhoda, unable to speak, pointed to the door of what Roger knew to be the night nursery. The superintendent wasted no time on further questions. He ran to the room and what he saw was indeed terrible.

Lady Bethesda, fully clothed, lay on the floor and round her neck was a loose stocking, possibly one of her own as it was similar to those she was wearing and to others hanging on the side of the cot by which she was lying. Her eyes and mouth were open, the former staring into space. Her cheeks were congested, with some make-up unnatural patchy.

Yeo removed the stocking and put his hand to her heart. There was no sign of life.

"Call the doctor immediately," he said to Carston. "Try it," he added to Allenby.

The latter knew what he meant. He knelt by the body and started artificial respiration, at which he was an expert. He was joined by Bellairs who had now arrived. Their efforts were too late. No sign of life or of recovering consciousness responded to their efforts.

Yeo looked slowly round the room, touching nothing. There was no sign of a struggle, though the bed coverlet had been dragged to the floor as though the woman had clutched at it when falling. With it had fallen a little suit, apparently out for the child to change into when he returned. The bed was a short one with rails to the top portion. On one rail hung the other similar stockings. Yeo went back to the landing.

"Who found her?" he asked Rhoda.

The girl pointed to Brigid who was still hysterically moaning with an occasional scream. She was in no condition to be questioned.

Yeo returned to the room just as Lord Bethesda, supported by Roger, reached the door and saw what had happened. The old man's legs refused to carry him farther. But for Roger's strong arm he would have collapsed.

"You cannot do anything," Roger said gently. "Better come to your room."

Half led, half carried, Lord Bethesda went to the main bedroom where he sank heavily into a chair.

"Dr. Strange will soon be here," Roger murmured. "I fear there is nothing I can do. Would you like to go to bed?"

"No," the old man said weakly. "Leave me. I will soon be better."

Glancing round the luxuriously appointed apartment Roger saw a flask of brandy on the dressing-table. He poured out a fair portion.

"Better take this," he said. "I will send Rhoda."

He found the girl outside. She had managed in some degree to calm the sobbing nurse and had taken her and little Ambrose to the day nursery. She had then returned to see if she could help her uncle.

"Who discovered it?" Roger asked her, repeating Yeo's question.

"Brigid," Rhoda said. She was shaking from the shock but she managed to keep control of herself in a wonderful way. "I saw her come in with Ambrose. She always takes him upstairs to change his things. Then I heard her scream. I ran up and I—I saw it, too."

Her voice broke, but she went bravely on—"Aunt Connie was lying—face downwards. I thought—I thought she had fainted. I turned her over. Then I noticed the stocking. I—I loosened it but I—I knew she was dead. Brigid screamed again and one of the detectives came up. I said he—had better fetch you. Then—I went to Brigid—" Rhoda broke off with a sob.

"It was a terrible shock for you, Rhoda," Roger said gently, "but you did all that was possible. I have taken your uncle to his room. You had better be with him till the doctor comes. But first I would like to see Brigid."

She led him to the day nursery where the nurse was still spasmodically sobbing.

"This is a very sad thing, Brigid," he said, "but we need your help. Do you think you can look after Ambrose for a few minutes, or would you like one of the ladies or one of the maids to be with you?"

"M-Merid" she muttered.

Merid was a chambermaid who normally assisted in looking after the little boy. Roger said she should come. He did not speak to Ambrose but put his hand softly on his head.

"Mummie ill?" the boy asked.

"Very, very ill," was the reply. "You must be good and very brave."

"Chief White Bull," Ambrose said, remembering the name Roger had called him.

"Yes, as brave as Chief White Bull." He moved to the door and then turned back.

"Did you meet or see anyone, Brigid, when you returned from your walk and came upstairs?"

"I s-saw one gentleman. I—I don't know his n-name. The one with the long hair and the b-beard."

Jeremiah!

"Where was he?"

"N-near the bottom of the stairs."

"Did you see him, Rhoda?"

"No. I was in my room. I saw Brigid and Ambrose pass the window. I did not go out until I heard the scream."

"How soon after?"

"Almost immediately."

"Then you ran up. There was no one about?"

"No one."

Yeo was still in the night nursery waiting impatiently for the doctor. His assistants were busy on their grim task, but when the thread of life is snapped human efforts are unavailing. He had asked everyone else to return to the dining-room.

He gazed frowningly out of the window. That this was a second murder there could be no doubt. The sheer audacity of the crime appalled him. Some of what were regarded as the best brains in the C.I.D. had come to the house to elucidate the murder of Ewen Jones and while they were there in full command, and almost under their very noses, this terrible thing had been done.

That the two crimes were connected there could be no reasonable doubt. If he failed to solve the first what would be thought of him were he equally baffled by the second? He could almost hear the sniggers of his underlings. His career would be ended. That must not happen. No one should leave the house until he had torn the truth from them.

Shut Lady Bethesda's mouth! Who had said that? Who had acted upon it—and why?

After what seemed a long time Dr. Strange arrived. He was visibly distressed by this further tragedy in the most eminent family he served. He entered the room and the efforts to restore animation ceased. He made an examination and declared life extinct. Yeo signalled Allenby and Bellairs to withdraw and explained how the body had been found and showed the stocking.

"How long has she been dead?" he asked the doctor who was already busy testing the limbs for rigor and taking the temperature of the corpse.

"About an hour," was the reply. "We cannot be more exact than that."

"Suffocation?"

"Undoubtedly."

"How long would that take?"

Strange pursed his lips. "When the blood-flow to the brain is stopped insensibility may be almost immediate, though life is not extinct. Strangling to cause death and the facial distortion takes longer."

"It must have been done by someone in the house," Yeo said. "Possibly by the same person who shot Ewen. The nearer I can get to the precise moment the more it will narrow down those who could be guilty."

"I see that. There is no sign of a blow so, unless she had taken a drug to cause insensibility, I should imagine someone from behind her slipped the stocking over her head and used great pressure. I can remove the body and make a further examination if you wish. I doubt it telling us much more."

"Perhaps tomorrow," Yeo said, "if it is necessary."

"How is Lord Bethesda?"

"Pretty near collapse."

"I will see him. The double shock might almost kill him, too."

"The photographer has done his job," Yeo said. "We might put her on the bed and I will take you to his lordship."

Rhoda came out of the room when the doctor went in. She met Yeo and Roger Bennion. The latter had been waiting to tell the superintendent what he had learned from her and Brigid.

"What were you doing all afternoon?" Yeo asked her.

"I was in my room most of the time," Rhoda said, "answering the telephone." She was more composed and spoke almost

141

normally. Attention to Brigid had in some measure helped her.

"There was no call for me?"

"No. If there had been I should have put it through at once. It is only an extension in the room you were using. They were mostly calls from friends and neighbours as the news about Ewen spread. I made notes of them. There were also a few callers after the vicar left. I sent them away as I thought you would no wish to be interrupted. I can give you their names."

"No visit or call from Jeremy?" Roger asked.

"No," she coloured. "I told him I would let him know when he could come."

"You did not see anyone go upstairs?" Yeo resumed.

"No one. Brigid met Mr. Dayton. At least I think that is whom she meant."

"I will see her. About the stockings, this is a similar one from the bedrail. Would you say it is Lady Bethesda's?"

Rhoda's hand trembled a little as she took it. "I should say it is."

"Would it be usual for her ladyship's stockings to be on the little boy's bedrail?"

"Quite usual. Brigid is a good needlewoman and my aunt often put stockings there if they needed mending. It was something for her to do while Ambrose was going to sleep."

She showed two places in the stocking that needed slight repair.

Dr. Strange did not spend long with Lord Bethesda. He murmured words of sympathy on this further shock and took his pulse.

"You would be better in bed," he said.

"I do not wish to go to bed just yet," Lord Bethesda replied in a low tone. "I shall have my things taken to another room."

Dr. Strange could understand that. It would be better for him to leave the twin-bedded room with all its associations and with his wife's many belongings in it.

"I will send a nurse along presently," he said. "She will help you. Have you been taking those special heart pills?"

"Not today. I had some brandy."

"You had better take two now." The doctor went to the dressing-table and picking up the bottle took two of the capsules. "Twelve left," he said. "Remember never more than two at a time, or six in a day at three hourly intervals, without my knowledge. I will send some more tomorrow or the next day."

He gave him the dose with some water and repeated such words of sympathy and condolence as were possible.

"I will look in again tonight."

He departed, but he was a great deal more worried than he allowed his patient to realise. Two brutal murders within a few hours. Was there a madman in the house or had someone a vendetta against the family? Was Lord Bethesda safe? Would there be an attack on the little boy? Another possibility occurred to him.

Strange's was a normal comfortable country practice. He had never met such appalling tragedies before. He again sought for Superintendent Yeo and found him and Roger Bennion together.

"How is Lord Bethesda?" the detective asked.

"Fairly comfortable. I am sending a nurse to be with him tonight and shall come in myself later on. Had you reached any conclusion in Ewen's case?"

"Rather early for conclusions in a house so full of unusual visitors," Yeo said stiffly.

"Of course, of course," the doctor murmured. "It is a terrible affair. I was wondering if you thought the same party responsible for both the crimes and if there is danger for anyone else."

The idea of further danger had not actually occurred to the harassed superintendent, though it might have done so when he had a little more time to consider matters. It was a very unpleasant thought.

"We can only proceed a step at a time," he said. "Have you any suggestion?"

"One thing has worried me," was the doctor's reply. "I do not believe very much in psychiatry. Those who practise it are too prone to lay down rules as though all human beings had the same reactions. In my experience they do not. A person of a sullen temperament who is continually reproved and repressed may harbour a feeling of resentment against the individual responsible for it. Some startling happening, such as a murder, may incite the idea of imitation. So you get the second crime."

143

Yeo stared at him. "You have someone in mind?" he asked.

"I have, but I doubt if I ought to give the name."

"The only person I can think of," Roger said, "who might conceivably fit your picture would be the girl Brigid. Am I right?"

"You are," the doctor admitted a little reluctantly. "I have observed her for some time and I think she does suffer from repression. I only suggest it is a case for investigation."

Yeo looked doubtful. "Would she—or anyone—having committed such a crime draw immediate attention to it by screaming the house down?"

"Not at all unlikely. Having been given the stockings to mend, a task she perhaps disliked, she could conceivably act in the manner described with one of them. Then, realising the horror of what she had done, there might be the hysterical reflex."

Yeo turned to Roger. "What do you think of that?"

"I should rule it out entirely," was the reply. "Dr. Strange may be correct in thinking the second crime was suggested or instigated by the first and committed by a different hand. But not by Brigid. He knows her better than I do, but what he regards as sullen resentment I should ascribe to a nervous desire to please a possibly difficult mistress. Apart however from her mentality, I do not think she had the opportunity for such an act. She was seen to come in and the screams followed almost immediately after. And we must remember the little boy was with her all the time. For her to attack the mother in such a way in front of him is unthinkable."

"I hope you are right," the doctor said a little testily.

21

Recriminations

There was at first silence in the dining-room when the company returned there as desired by the superintendent. It was not only horror that stilled their voices, there was also an indefinite sense of fear and suspicion. Was it possible that one of them had been guilty of this second murder—and perhaps also of the first?

No one talked of leaving. They knew the police would not allow it. They realised they must see the matter through.

The women could not express any real regret or regard for Lady Bethesda. They had resented her manner to them. It had been aloof or—if she spoke—condescending. Perhaps, too, there had been some feeling of envy on their part. They understood her grandfather had been a barman in a public-house. Why should she adopt such airs of superiority? Yet, despite all that, they were unutterably shocked at her fate. Who could have done so foul a thing to her?

The same feeling of uncertainty and apprehension possessed the men. Publicity is the breath of life to politicians, but it must be publicity of the right kind. To be mixed up in this terrible affair could do them no good. The death of Ewen Jones was bad enough, but the callous slaughter of their hostess was infinitely worse. It would create an appalling sensation and might do them incalculable harm.

The Party chiefs would assuredly learn of the meeting of the Ginger Group. They would probe every detail of it. The Trade Unions also would want to know what their representatives were doing there. Even those who were innocent of complicity in the crimes would find black marks against their names and would probably lose official recognition.

The fact that the luncheon table had not been cleared added in some measure to their discomfort. They had been lavishly entertained and there seemed a silent reproach in the disordered debris of the meal. Ossie Henshaw was perhaps the one exception. He had rejoined the rest of the party, and as the port decanter was not empty he fortified himself with another glass.

Each, perhaps, was waiting for others to say something. The long silence was at last broken by Fred Gibbons. He had been walking restlessly up and down the room and he stopped in front of Bill Ruttle.

"Why the hell did you tell Superintendent Yeo what we had been talking about in here?" he demanded.

"I did not," was the reply. "He already knew."

"Then who told him?"

They both looked at their companions to discover the culprit.

"It must have been you, Gwen," Gibbons said accusingly. "You were called out before they saw Ruttle and myself."

"It was not me," she replied. "I did not know what you had been talking about and I don't now."

"You were sitting at that desk," Ruttle declared, pointing at it. "Taking it down."

"Taking what down?" she retorted. "I did not hear what you were saying."

"Then what were you writing?" Gibbons sceptically enquired.

"I was writing what I remembered of Ewen's speech while it was fresh in my memory, and what you all said about it."

"Where is it? Can you show it us?"

"No. They took my notebook for a record. They promised to return it but have not yet done so."

"What did you want it for?" Ruttle asked.

"I had to do something. It might be useful when I wrote about it."

"Ewen's obituary?" Gibbons sneered.

"Possibly."

"That would not prove you did not hear something and told them about it," Boyne remarked.

"Don't bully Gwen," Ossie Henshaw said. "If you want to know, I told them."

"What the devil had to do with you?" Bill Ruttle demanded fiercely.

"Nothing—or everything," Ossie replied. "We want to know who shot Ewen—or don't we?"

"You should know, if anyone," Gibbons sneered.

"What do you mean by that?" the captain returned.

"It was obvious to most of us that you had a considerable motive for disliking him," said the M.P.

"So it was you who told them the lies that Ewen had come between me and Sandra?"

"Were they lies?" Ruttle asked loudly. Everyone else was

146

listening. Were they getting the true explanation of the affair?

"I refuse to discuss my wife with any tub-thumping mobsters," Ossie said warmly. "I told them no lies. I suggested they should ask you what was meant by the remarks I could not help hearing. That certain things never happened; that you must keep your mouths shut and make your wives keep theirs shut too. Also that Lady Bethesda must be silenced. You – one or both of you—would appear to have done that very effectively!"

Both Gibbons and Ruttle were red with anger.

"If you dare say that again," the latter exclaimed threateningly, "I will knock your head off."

"No need to say it again," Henshaw retorted. "The police are as capable of putting two and two together as most people. You cannot deny you used those words, or words to that effect."

"You devil!" Ruttle cried, taking a step towards him, his fist raised. Sandra was watching her husband, yet there was no sign of what she was thinking. She knew he was no coward but he was no match for Big Bill if it came to fighting. The intervention came, however, from an unexpected quarter. Old "Jeremiah" Dayton moved between them, his hands aloft in protest.

"Nothing will be gained by our quarrelling among ourselves," he said. "It is possible you are all right and yet all wrong. Certain words were used that might have had a meaning quite different to what Captain Henshaw supposed. Ruttle and Gibbons may have misconstrued certain attentions paid by our poor friend Ewen to one of his guests. I suggest the explanation of the terrible crimes may lie in quite a different quarter."

"And what might that be?" Gibbons sneered.

"Are there not strange servants in the house? Some of them I believe are foreign. I cannot say what motives they may have had. That is for the police to find out. Those who know they are innocent have no need to be afraid. Let them pray that the truth may be discovered."

"Mr. Dayton is right," Gwennie Wren said. "We can each tell what we know to be true. The question of proof is not in our hands."

"I only said what I knew to be true," Ossie muttered. "It has not been contradicted."

"What I said was true, too," Gibbons commented. "Nor has it been contradicted, only refused to be discussed."

Ossie might have made a hot rejoinder, but there was a sudden silence. The door opened and Superintendent Yeo, grim and purposeful, strode into the room.

22

Conspiracy Of Silence

"I do not want to make a speech," Yeo began. "You all know what has happened. The murder of Ewen Jones on Saturday night by shooting has been followed this afternoon by the murder of Lady Bethesda by strangling. It does not follow that both crimes were by the same hand, but it would be strange if there were two murderers in the house at the same time, unless they were acting in collusion. I look to you all for your assistance in clearing up these crimes; to all, it may be, except those guilty of them. It may well be that the murderer or murderers are in this room now."

All eyes were on him. What did he know? Had he learned at in the brief time that had elapsed since the new tragedy had been discovered? He could not be sure as to the criminal or he would not have spoken as he did.

Roger Bennion had returned with him and had taken a seat by the door. The two inspectors, Allenby and Bellairs, stood not far off. Sergeant Carston, notebook in hand, sat at the desk Gwennie Wren had previously used.

It was an impressive proceeding and a shiver seemed to pass through the company when Yeo made his statement—as well it might. He had decided it would be best to see them all in this way in the first place, though individual interrogations might follow. There was silence for a perceptible time.

"Has any one of you anything to say?" Yeo asked.

Then Boyne spoke. He was the man who had declared that Ewen's

148

suggestions seemed like Russia to him. He put forward Jeremiah's theory.

"We are shocked almost beyond words by what has happened," he said. "I am sure we would help you if we could, but I believe there is a considerable domestic staff, some strange to the house. Is it proved beyond doubt that none of them is implicated?"

There was a general murmur of assent and relief when this question was put. It seemed such a reasonable suggestion.

"I am sure none of our men is concerned," Mrs. Boyne added. "But aliens—"

"I need hardly say that the idea as to the domestic staff has been well considered," Yeo replied. "As a matter of fact Inspector Bellairs was in the servants' quarters all the afternoon taking statements and checking references. They were all present and not one of them left their quarters during the time that is vital to us, from half-past two until four o'clock, between which hours Lady Bethesda was murdered. That is why these luncheon things have not been cleared away or tea served. We are also satisfied that no one from outside gained entrance as the doors were guarded."

He paused. As no one spoke he added—"It is perhaps fair that I should say no suspicion attaches to Captain Henshaw, at least for the death of Lady Bethesda. At my request he remained in the billiards room with one of my officers, pending the receipt of a telephone message that has not yet reached us."

"For which relief much thanks," Ossie drawled.

"No information?" Yeo asked, again looking round the room. There was silence. Perhaps they remembered the maxim qui s'excuse s'accuse and preferred to leave the talking to him. "If you do not help me voluntarily," the superintendent proceeded, "I must ask some questions. When after lunch you gentlemen were discussing matters among yourselves, who was it said Lady Bethesda's mouth must be shut?"

The women looked uneasily at their men. Captain Henshaw's hint was the first they had heard of such a thing. Its significance was obvious and it seemed to be true.

"I rather think it was our friend Bert Doodell," Gibbons said quietly. "But there was no thought of violence in it. I am sure of that."

"I said nothing of the sort," Doodell declared warmly. "I never even thought of it. It was Gibbons who suggested if there was any enquiry about Ewen's speech we must pretend it never happened. All I said was the women were present when he spoke as well as ourselves. I was thinking of our wives, not Lady Bethesda. If anyone mentioned her, it was Gibbons himself."

"No," Gibbons said. "It was not me. It might have been Ruttle."

"Certainly not!" Big Bill shouted.

"Her mouth has been shut," Yeo said sternly. "I want to know who first suggested it."

There were at once charges, counter-charges and denials.

"You were present, Captain Henshaw," Yeo said. "Perhaps you can tell us."

"It was Ruttle," Henshaw replied. "His voice was louder than the others."

"That is right," Joe Edmonds declared. Edmonds was Ewen's friend, and if anyone really grieved for him it was he. "Ruttle said she hated us and would make mischief if she could."

Then others remembered the same words. Big Bill looked furious.

"We were all talking about Gibbons's absurd suggestions," he said. "How could we pretend a thing had never happened when besides ourselves there were so many witnesses to it? Lord and Lady Bethesda, Captain and Mrs. Henshaw, Gwennie Wren, and Major Bennion? If I mentioned one name it was merely to show how ridiculous it was. I had nothing against Lady Bethesda and I never saw her again."

"It is unfortunate the idea was acted on so promptly," Yeo said icily. "Did any of you see Lady Bethesda during the afternoon?"

"I did," Winkworth replied. "I went to my overcoat in the cloakroom to get my tobacco pouch. She came down the stairs with the little boy and his nurse. They were going out for a walk. I presume she went upstairs again though I did not see her. I did not speak to her."

"That is true," Mrs. Winkworth said. "Mrs. Doodell and I were sitting by the window and saw them start off. Lady Bethesda was there and waved to them."

"Quite Mrs. Doodell nodded.

"Did you go out of the room again?" Yeo asked Winkworth.

"I did not."

That, if true, seemed to exculpate him. How many more could be eliminated?

"Which of you went upstairs?" Yeo asked very deliberately.

There was no answer.

"You are not being co-operative," the superintendent said sternly. "I have reason to know some of you left this room. It can hardly have been done without anyone observing it."

"I went to the cloakroom," Edmonds said, "but for a different reason from Winkworth's. I did not go upstairs or see anyone."

"What about you, Mr. Dayton?"

"Eh?" asked "Jeremiah," putting his hand to his ear.

"You went upstairs, didn't you?" Yeo said more loudly.

"Yes," was the reply.

"Why did you do that?"

Dayton hesitated. Every eye was now on him. Could it be old "Jeremiah" after all? Of course he was a bit crazy; had he heard a call to start the doom he so often predicted? His denial soon came.

"Gibbons told me we should shortly be leaving and he had already packed his bag. So I went up to pack mine."

"At what time was this?"

"I do not know exactly. It didn't take long. I passed the nurse and the little boy as I came down. Soon after that there were the screams."

That tallied with what Brigid had said, though it did not prove his innocence. Yeo turned swiftly to Gibbons.

"So you went upstairs, too?"

"I did," Gibbons replied. "Ruttle told me he had done so and I thought it a good idea to be ready to go."

"Yet you did not mention it and would not have done so had not Mr. Dayton told me."

"I should have done so in private," Gibbons said smoothly. "I was waiting for Ruttle to speak. I did not see Lady Bethesda or anyone else. It would not have helped you."

151

"And you, Mr. Ruttle," Yeo accused, "you also had been up there and were silent about it. How do you explain that? Had you been putting your suggestion about Lady Bethesda into effect?"

"Certainly not," Big Bill said hotly. "You have no right to suggest such a thing. I did not see Lady Bethesda or go near the room where she was found. I did tell Gibbons I had packed. As Dayton said, it did not take long."

"Was that before or after your interview with me?"

"Immediately after," Ruttle said.

"Yet I had distinctly told you you could not go."

"I meant to stand on my rights," was the defiant reply. "We are not people who can disappear. You could always find me if you wanted me."

"I wanted you here just then," Yeo retorted.

"If I had harmed Lady Bethesda in any way," Ruttle asked angrily, "should I have told anyone I had been up there?"

"That is not for me to say," Yeo replied. "You did not admit it until I got it from others."

Then he addressed the company in general.

"Is this another conspiracy of silence? I would remind you all of your responsibility in the matter. If you withhold evidence you may be charged as accessories, and that in a case of deliberate murder is a very serious thing. I asked if anyone left the room and with two exceptions you were all silent. We now know that three others not only did so but went to the bedroom floor. Yet not one of you had a word to say about it. Perhaps you do not like to speak in front of your friends. I will question you separately and I hope you will realise more fully your duty in the matter."

He paused a moment and turned to his assistant by the door. "Inspector Allenby, go to the rooms occupied by Mr. Gibbons, Mr. Ruttle and Mr. Dayton and see if all their things are packed as they say. I will wait till you return. You might also look in the other rooms and see if the packing there has been done, too."

"I did not say every little thing was packed," Ruttle muttered.

"I am not sure as to my hair brushes," Gibbons remarked.

"Jeremiah" said nothing.

152

As Allenby left the room, Rhoda slipped in. She saw Roger and told him her uncle would like to speak to him.

23

Roger's Question

Lord Bethesda was still in the room where Roger had left him. The room he had shared with his unfortunate wife. It was a handsome spacious apartment with lofty panelled walls. Many of the Priors of old no doubt lived in comfort whatever austerities they may have deemed good for their weaker brothers. There was the incongruity in its present furnishings as was shown in her ladyship's room downstairs. The twin beds, some distance apart, were of the good Tottenham Court Road brass of some years ago. Each had a silken coverlet embroidered with a golden coronet with the appropriate number of knobs. The large dressing-table of Regency design carried a profusion of bottles and beauty aids. Two spacious wardrobes with mirror panels were of Victorian walnut. The Chinese carpet was soft and irreproachable. Near the dressing-table stood an escritoire that bore on it three large photographs in heavy silver frames showing Master Ambrose at different stages in his young life. A Recamier bed-sofa and chairs of many styles ancient and modern added variety if not dignity to the room. The fine old basket grate with a wrought-iron Suffolk fire-back set in a finely carved marble mantel had not been removed, but was screened by an electric fire with many bars. Neither the old Welsh Lion nor his lady would have claimed aesthetic tastes. If they pleased themselves what else mattered?

Lord Bethesda was seated at a substantial circular table. He was clothed as before except that he had removed his coat and collar and tie and had donned a dressing-gown. Apparently he was waiting for the nurse the doctor had promised to send. He looked more composed than he had previously done. The pills the doctor had insisted on his taking had been effective.

"Don't wait, Rhoda," he said to his niece.

"Let me know if you want me," she replied. "I shall be close handy." The old man nodded and waved Roger to a chair.

"Well, Major Bennion," he said, "how are they getting on downstairs?" His voice was almost normal.

"Superintendent Yeo is going carefully into things," Roger answered. "There is a good deal of conflicting evidence. Your son certainly had rivals if not open enemies."

"After what Sir Cowdrey Hood of the Colonial Office told me of your success in such matters I should have thought you would at least have discovered who killed my son." The words were spoken in a faintly ironic manner.

"Maybe I have, sir. But some process of elimination is necessary to prevent error. That takes time."

"How far has the elimination gone?"

"I am afraid I cannot tell you that. The first question is whether anyone in the room could have fired the shots. If not, we have to consider those who were not in the room."

"Who were they?"

"There seem to have been five. Captain Henshaw, Bill Ruttle and Fred Gibbons. Also 'Jeremiah' Dayton and myself: 'Jeremiah' and I were together in the billiards room until we heard the screams. I hope that eliminates us."

"What of the others?"

"That is more difficult After a game of snooker with me Henshaw went into the garden and came in wet. He complained it was hot in the house and wandered towards the river. He says he took shelter in the hut. The only person he saw was your gardener, Floss. I think we can eliminate Floss."

"I am sure you can. But why was Floss there? Did he see anyone?"

"He went into the garden on the chance of seeing me about the promise of the house your son had."

"Did he see anyone?"

"Apparently only Henshaw and a man from the village called Luke Catling. We have pretty well cleared Catling. And also Rhoda."

"Little Rhoda!" Bethesda exclaimed. "Surely no one suspected her?"

154

"I would not say that. She had opportunity for each of the crimes."

"That is unthinkable." The idea seemed to shake the old man. "I may agree," Roger said, "but the police must consider all possibilities. Henshaw is perhaps Yeo's chief suspect."

"He was Ewen's friend."

"Or his wife was."

"I know what you mean," Bethesda murmured. "No one saw anybody at or near the window?"

"Apparently not."

"What about Gibbons and Ruttle?"

"Gibbons told us he retired to his bedroom and fell asleep. Ruttle says he was in the study preparing a speech. Both reappeared shortly after the shooting. Neither has an alibi."

"I have been here all day and know so little of what has been happening," the old man said. "But you implied you had ideas of your own apart from Yeo's suspicions. What are they?"

"Should I not leave it to Yeo?"

"I would rather you told me."

"You are sure you wish that?"

"Quite sure. It is why I sent for you. I have not much time and the truth must be told, whatever the consequences."

"But perhaps when you are feeling stronger?"

"Who knows that I shall ever feel stronger than I now am?" Roger was silent for some moments. It was one of the hardest decisions of his life. But he could see the old man was in earnest and meant every word he said.

"You would not wish the innocent to suffer?"

"Indeed I would not," Bethesda replied.

"I do not pretend I have absolute proof," Roger said, "but if insist I will tell you my conclusion and what led to it."

"I do insist," was the calm return.

Roger did not immediately reply. He knew what he had to say and that it must be said, yet he wished there was some other way in which it could be done. Then he spoke quietly but with no lack of confidence.

"There were two interruptions at critical moments when I was asking if the chart I had drawn as to where you all were sitting during the TV play was correct. I requested everyone to return to the seats they had occupied before the crime was discovered. After a little question as to where Rhoda sat this was done. You were then in seat number 23 and Lady Bethesda in seat number 22. I asked you if that was right. You said 'Yes, except'—Lady Bethesda interrupted to say that of course you did not know where everyone sat as some moved and some came in late. There was room for all."

"I remember."

"Then the police arrived and I handed over to them. I have told you more or less of their enquiries, which are still proceeding. The second interruption was when you were being interviewed this afternoon by Yeo. He asked if I had any questions to put to you. I returned to the same point. If Lady Bethesda occupied seat 22 she must have brushed past you when she switched on the light. You were about to reply when there was the scream from upstairs and we heard of her death."

Roger paused. There was no reply. He went on—"I put the question for a third time in a more definite form? Am I right in believing that during the showing of the film you were in seat 22 and Lady Bethesda in seat 23, the one nearest the light and nearest the door?"

"You are right," was the reply in a tone as quiet as his own.

"Thank you. I think you meant to tell me so when we were first interrupted. It would seem a trivial detail but it was of vast consequence. The person in seat 23 by the door must almost surely have known if anyone went out. The person in seat 22 absorbed by the play, might not."

There was a nod, but no audible reply.

"The person in seat 2 might even have slipped out unobserved."

Still there was no reply.

"Lady Bethesda told us she switched on the light. She could hardly have done that in the dark without pushing past you had she been in seat 22. It is almost within reach from seat 23."

Another nod. But no answer.

"That was what first turned my thoughts in a certain direction. Naturally I shared Yeo's suspicions of those who were not in the room, whose names I have given you. If they were innocent, could there be a motive to justify my own terrible and almost incredible misgiving?"

Roger paused. Bethesda, with bowed head, waited for him to proceed.

"Unhappily there was."

"Go on," the old man said.

"I would spare you pain, sir, if I could, but it is not possible. Hate and jealousy are among the most compelling of human emotions. I will not suggest that. Lady Bethesda hated Ewen, though she certainly did not love him. Perhaps his greatest fault in her eyes was that on your death he became the new Baron Bethesda. By marrying you she acquired a title. If Ewen were removed your title would pass to her son. Otherwise he would remain Ambrose Jones. A worthy enough name but not suiting her desires."

Again there was no reply. Having got so far in his unpleasant task Roger was able to speak more easily.

"Titles in these days mean little to many people but to some they stand for a great deal. There have been many cases in history where a stepmother has acted in a similar way for a similar reason. I was visiting Corfe in Dorset recently where there is a memorial marking the spot where Queen Efrida stabbed King Edward, her stepson, while offering him a drink, so that her own son might become king. I am sorry to pain you with this long statement but you asked me to do so. There are, of course, other factors that guided me, but if you can assure me I am entirely wrong I may not have to repeat to Superintendent Yeo what I have said to you. His suspicions are still elsewhere. But we agreed we could not let an innocent person suffer."

"Go on," the old man murmured again. "Let me hear it all."

"No one can have been so well aware as Lady Bethesda of the shooting that was to take place in the play. She had seen it before. No one else could have known just where Ewen would sit when he was present. She also knew that the windows and the curtains met exactly behind the TV set. Would a visitor be likely to be aware of that?"

There was no reply.

157

Roger went on: "After the arrival of the police she went upstairs with you while everyone else remained below. That gave her an opportunity to dispose of the gun, if she had not already done so. It was placed in Gwennie Wren's room and Lady Bethesda knew there was a break in Gwen's friendship with Ewen. The back sheet of a letter Gwen had written her was used for a message intended to mislead. On it was typed 'He was ambitious so—'. 'So I slew him' completes the quotation. Whether it was meant to incriminate Gwen further, or whether it was to cast suspicion on other M.P.s, I cannot say. Lady Bethesda had the best opportunity to use Rhoda's machine on which it was typed."

A silent nod was the only response.

"It is said we should speak no ill of the dead," Roger continued more slowly. "It could not harm them but it might be terribly distressing for the living. But you did not stop me. It is fair to say that there are no finger-prints on the gun except those of Miss Wren. She found it among her clothes and brought it to me. I have as yet no proof that Lady Bethesda possessed a gun, but Scotland Yard has considerable resources in tracing such things."

"What was the gun like?" Those were Bethesda's first words for a considerable time.

"A short five-chambered revolver of the Colt type. It could almost be concealed in the hand. Three shots found in the body match the two remaining in the weapon."

"It was Connie's gun," her husband said.

24

The Inevitable Sequel

There was a long silence. The old man who had suffered such terrible shocks in so short a time still sat in his chair, his eyes closed and, his face, mask-like, void of expression. The admission as to the gun completed the case as far as Roger was concerned. He had no more to say on that issue and was grieved rather than exultant at the accuracy of his deductions. He waited for Bethesda to speak. At last came the poignant question—"As you have discovered so much, Major Bennion, I suppose you are also convinced as to who killed my wife?"

"I am most regrettably forced to a certain conclusion," Roger replied. "An inevitable sequel."

There was another lengthy silence, again broken by the older man.

"I had better tell you about it. I would like you to understand. When we married, the cynics said I wanted Connie's money and she wanted my title. That was true in a way, but not all of the truth. I do not claim to be better than other men and of course I do not pretend to the romantic passion of youth. Yet at first there was, or there seemed to be, real affection between us. We each felt the other would help to what we desired. But it may be we desired different things. Gold, they tell us, cannot corrode, but it can rot the soul."

He was speaking slowly, choosing his words with some care. Roger did not interrupt.

"I will not weary you with a description of our early days together. I had ideals when I was younger and I still had them, but I was cloyed and pampered until I lost my zest. Then I was ill. I was surrounded with luxury on a scale I had never dreamed of. I suppose I was like an opium smoker whose energies are sapped by the dream world in which he lives. The more I resisted the stronger became my chains. Her arguments seemed so convincing. I still supported my Party, but it was in a passive rather than an active manner."

He paused. But not for long.

"When Ambrose was born there was a change. She was utterly devoted to the boy. She was still kind, too kind, too thoughtful, for me. The change was towards Ewen. Previously they had got on well enough, but then she made him feel he was not welcome here. When I was again ill this grew more apparent. He still came at times to see me; sometimes alone, sometimes with friends. She did not encourage it. I must not weary you with that."

He paused again. He had said enough for Roger to see how the woman with the money had dominated him.

"When Ewen suggested having his friends here to form what he termed his Ginger Group I thought she would object. To my surprise and pleasure she did not. She said she thought I would enjoy it and she would do all she could to make the party a success. You know what happened. I was startled and upset by some of the things Ewen told us he meant to urge on our leaders. I did not think they would be adopted, but we need not go into that.

"My wife also appeared vexed by them and by the acrimonious comments of some of the guests. She suggested that to prevent quarrelling on the second evening we should all see that TV play, a repeat of one we had had before. I agreed....

"When it was discovered that Ewen had been shot I was too shocked to realise the importance of the precise seats we had occupied. I was in a way aware of the fact that she had left the room for a short time. I had been deeply interested in the story and a hostess might well have matters to attend to. I gave such things no thought until a remark she made when we were upstairs brought them suddenly to my mind like an evil dream: 'It is of course very sad, but the title does not become extinct. Ambrose will make a better Lord Bethesda than Ewen would ever have done. I will see to that.'

"Those were her words. The room was dark. I could not see her face but the satisfaction in her voice was unmistakable. For long I lay awake. The idea was horrible. I tried to put it from me. It could not be true."

He was speaking half to Roger, half to himself. There came a silence longer than before. Was there more to come?

"The gun?" Roger said softly, as a question.

"Yes, the gun," the old man went on, as though roused from a reverie. "It is strange how things so disconnected may shape our lives. When her father Josiah Marden bought this place he did not make himself popular. He objected to people using that footpath between the garden and the river. He said that by an old deed it was part of his property. The villagers swore there had always been a right of way. It was a sort of lovers' walk. Marden declared such use must stop. He put up notices that it was private property; trespassers forbidden. That meant a wide detour. As fast as he put up his notices they were pulled down and thrown into the river. He then erected a stout fence from each side of the garden to the water's edge enclosing the part he claimed as his. One night the fences were broken up and burnt. There were arrests and lawsuits followed. Marden lost the day. Old married couples swore they had used that path in their courting days; no one ever questioned their right.

160

"It was then that Connie bought her revolver. She and her father were afraid the angry villagers might attack the house. She told me this after we were married. I saw the weapon one day in the bottom drawer of that desk of hers. It was in a leather case. I advised her to get rid of it. She laughed and said there were too many burglars about; it might still be useful. I said if she used it there might be more danger for her than anyone else. She assured me she had practised with it and was a good shot.

"I did not know of this old quarrel until I came to live here. I was fairly well received though I was conscious of an under current of hostility. I found that Sir Godfrey Nokes whose family had owned the place for generations and who sold it to Marden had allowed cricket on the big lawn. Marden forbade it. I gave permission for it to be used again. I wished to be friendly with everyone. But soon after Ambrose was born Connie begged me—or ordered me—to stop it. I had parts of the common turfed and rolled and gave them a pavilion. . . ."

He made a gesture as though to dismiss bygone affairs.

"This morning—this morning, though it seems so long ago—I got up as soon as it was light to see if the gun was still in her drawer. I thought she was asleep. The case was there—but it was empty."

The old man's voice was weakening. The strain was telling on him. But without prompting he went on to the most horrible part of his story.

"I turned towards my bed. She had been watching me. 'What is the matter?' she asked. What could I say? I was proud of Ewen; I loved him, but I was a weak old coward. I wanted to think. I muttered I could not sleep and got back into my bed. What must I do? Could I accuse my own wife?"

Once again he stopped. Roger indeed felt sorry for him. It was little wonder he had been prostrated, though it had been attributed to a different cause. But that was not all.

"Throughout the morning she was most kind to me. She would hardly leave my side. Yet I knew—and she knew I knew. But I could not say a word. The end came soon after lunch, shortly before Strange called, earlier than we expected him. She said I must sleep and I should feel better. She would give me my pills. I generally took them dissolved in a glass of wine; I was never to take more than two. Through the mirror I saw her drop in at least six. She brought me the glass.... I said put it down; I would take it presently. She left

161

the room. I slipped out of bed and poured the stuff down the wash-basin. Then I got back and pretended to be asleep, the empty glass by my side... ."

He was relating it in an unemotional tone, almost as though he was an onlooker at something that happened to someone else. Then his voice grew more bitter.

"It was horribly clear. Strange had often said two pills would stimulate the heart, more would over-stimulate it and might be fatal. She had shot Ewen and she meant to get rid of me. Then our innocent little Ambrose would indeed be Lord Bethesda. I had not long to live in any case, but she could not wait. No doubt it was safer for her to silence me. It was all so easy. No one would suspect her. Even Strange would hardly be surprised.

"When he came he asked if I had taken any pills and I said No. He seemed to think there should be more in the bottle. Connie was there. If my reply surprised her she did not show it. Perhaps she thought I had forgotten; perhaps she thought she had not given me enough. If so, two more should help! She asked if I might see the detectives. Strange said yes, if it was necessary and I had had my sleep.

"Then I was left and again I pretended to sleep. She had seen the nurse take Ambrose out. She came back here and tiptoed across the floor to look at me. Then she crept away to the night nursery as she often did.

There was another pause. Roger did not speak. The old man must tell his story in his own way.

"I did not sleep. Who would? I got up and dressed but remained barefoot. I went to the nursery. The door was ajar. I did not know exactly what I meant to do. But Ambrose was my son as well as hers. I must not leave him to the care of a murderess....

"The way was made clear for me. She had carried some stockings into the room but one had fallen to the floor. I picked it up. She was bending over the bed, humming to herself. She did not hear me. I put the stocking over her head, round her neck. She struggled, but only for a few moments. I held on and drew it tighter—and tighter....

"Then I came back here and finished dressing. I called to Rhoda that I would see the superintendent. I meant—in the end—to tell him what I had done—and why. But, as you said, we were interrupted. . ."

He stopped. It was truly a terrible story. The woman was already dead before he came down to face his questioners, not killed while he was doing so. No one had a better opportunity; no one a more compelling reason.

"That is all. You have justified Hood's belief in you, Major Bennion. Now I suppose it is your duty to arrest me?"

"That is not my duty," Roger said, "though it may be for others. What is your wish?"

"I only wish to sleep."

"If I leave you to sleep will you first write out what you have told me? Not all of it, but enough to save other people from suspicion?"

"I will. I can promise you that. One other thing I want to say. I made a will some while ago leaving all I had to Rhoda. It is not much, but she is a good girl. Of course, Ambrose will be more than adequately provided for. I also said in the event of my wife's death before he became of age I would like Rhoda to be the boy's guardian. I do not know what made me add that. Perhaps it was some sort of premonition."

"You know she hopes to marry Jeremy Valiance?" Roger asked.

"She has not told me but I guessed. He is a good fellow. I am happy about it."

Roger rose to go. The old man stood up, too.

"I thank you for your help, Major Bennion. Keep an eye on Ambrose if you can. I do not know if you care to shake my hand?"

Roger took the wrinkled hand in both of his.

"I will."

25

The Best Possible Ending

"How is he?" Rhoda asked. "Shall I go to him?"

She had been waiting on the landing and came forward as Roger left the room.

163

"Not yet," he replied. "When is the nurse coming?"

"She 'phoned a little while ago. She had heard from Dr. Strange but she is busy on a case. It may be two or three hours before she can get here. She told him so."

"That should be soon enough. Your uncle has some writing to do and then he wants to go to sleep. No one is to disturb him unless he rings. What is happening downstairs?"

"I don't exactly know. I think Mr. Yeo finished talking to them in the dining-room and is now seeing them separately in the study. Do you think—do you think he will discover the truth? I never thought such dreadful things could happen."

There was a sob in her voice. He put a hand gently on her shoulder.

"You have been a grand girl, Rhoda. Few could have done all you have done, and been so brave. Yes, Yeo will discover the truth. You must keep your courage to the end. I believe you and Jeremy will soon be together. I told your uncle about it. He was not surprised and said it made him very happy. How is little Ambrose?"

"He is frightened. I do not think he quite understands. I promised he should sleep with me tonight and that seemed to comfort him."

"It is the best thing you could have done. Thank God there are such girls as you. See that no one disturbs your uncle. I will wait for a time in your office, if I may. I don't wish to disturb Yeo just yet. You will find me there if you want me."

She nodded. He went down the stairs and she returned to the room to be with the boy.

Was he doing right? That was the question Roger asked him self as he sat alone beside the desk that bore the typewriter that had played its small part in the drama that had just been unfolded

Lord Bethesda's story had only confirmed the theory he had already formed, filling in details at which he could only guess. He believed every word of it. The proof was overwhelming. But – was he doing right?

The old Welsh Lion had lived a wonderful life. Born in the humblest circumstances, when the miners' existence had often been truly pitiable, he had risen by his own exertions to a position he bad never dreamed of. He had fought for the under-dog and had been fully trusted by his fellows who had sent him to parliament with vast majorities. Finally came the reward of a peerage.

That, and the marriage that followed it, had been the beginning of tragedy. Gold can rot the soul. He had pronounced his own epitaph.

Had he, Roger Bennion, done right? Never before had been faced with such a problem. Some might say he ought to have told Yeo all his thoughts and fears. But he was there in no official capacity. The police were bound to pursue their investigation in their own way. There were grave reasons for suspicion in other directions. They surely should be examined?

Purists might contend that the law must be aided without sentiment and regardless of consequences. But suppose he had stressed that apparently trivial point as to the seats occupied by Lord and Lady Bethesda. It would not have saved Ewen's life. Nor would it have saved Lady Bethesda. She would not have hanged, though, if ever a woman deserved hanging, the one who in cold blood murdered a stepson and tried to murder her husband surely did. Short of capital punishment she would have spent the rest of her life in prison. But his theory would not have been established without the husband's testimony. Would that testimony have been forthcoming had not the husband taken steps to save the little boy from the influence of a murderess?

Lord Bethesda, knowing he had not long to live, was willing to sacrifice the few months that might remain to him to do what he felt to be just and right. Was he wrong?

Realising what was in the old man's mind ought he, Roger Bennion, to rush to the superintendent with his story so that there might be an arrest with a painful trial and a worthy life ended in shame? The Welsh Lion did not wish to live. The law allows a man to kill in self-defence. Was not that what he had actually done? Was it not better that he should go to his last sleep in his own way?

Roger was still pondering the problem when the telephone bell rang. He lifted the receiver.

"I wish to speak to Superintendent Yeo."

"What name please?"

"Inspector Wingate of Scotland Yard."

"He is engaged at present. I am Major Bennion. Can I give him a message? I suppose it has to do with Captain Henshaw?"

"That's right. Since it is you, Major Bennion, I think a message will do. I went to the hotel but there was some delay, as the manager

165

was out. I had to wait for his return as it was to him that Henshaw had spoken. When he came in he took me to the room. The gun was there all right, just as Henshaw had described."

"I will give the message, Inspector Wingate," Roger said. "I do not think the superintendent will be surprised as he is on the verge of quite a different solution of the matter."

"Good," was the reply with a laugh. "So Yeo gets his man—as usual."

That, if necessary, would put Henshaw in the clear. Better luck in some ways than he deserved, but he had still to have his reckoning with Sandra. Unless Roger was much in error, he had lost her, and it certainly served him right. She could return to her old job; what would happen to her scheming husband only time could tell. She had stood by him in swearing to his innocence of the crime, but he had not hesitated to call her a liar and accuse her of philandering when he thought it served his purpose. Not a nice man, Oswald Henshaw.

Roger wrote Wingate's message slowly and then, without hurry, took it to the adjacent room where the harassed superintendent was still questioning one by one the angry M.P.s and their wives.

He handed it to the man for whom it was meant. Yeo read it at a glance and tossed it on one side. At that moment he was tackling Fred Gibbons.

"You," he said, "admit you were opposed to the proposals put forward by Ewen Jones. You did not join the party in the TV room and could not truthfully account for how you spent your evening. You declared you had gone to your bedroom to finish reading a book, yet you could not say what the book was about. You then said you had been asleep! It was about that time Ewen Jones was killed. Your shoes showed you had been in the garden. This afternoon you urged your friends to pretend it never happened, referring to the speech made by Ewen Jones. You men must be silent and the women must keep their mouths shut. That included Lady Bethesda. You led me to believe you had never been upstairs, but I discovered that was untrue. And at that time Lady Bethesda was murdered. Have you any further statement to make?"

Gibbons had lost his air of easy assurance. He was perspiring freely and looked very worried, as a man faced by such an indictment might well do. He mopped his face with his handkerchief.

"I have nothing more to say. Possibly I erred in some details but I

166

never thought my innocent actions could be so distorted. I know nothing whatever of the death of Ewen Jones or of Lady Bethesda. That I swear."

"What are the distortions?" Yeo demanded.

So it went on. Roger sitting again by the door felt it was a little unfair to let these men suffer such prolonged discomfort. Yet he was not particularly sorry for them. He must not hurry things.

At long last Rhoda once more appeared. She beckoned him to come to her.

"The nurse has arrived," she whispered. "Uncle appears asleep. She cannot wake him."

Roger nodded and went to Yeo's side.

"You had better come," he said. "It is Lord Bethesda. The nurse cannot rouse him."

Without a word Yeo followed him. From Roger's manner he realised the matter was serious and urgent. Silently they went up the stairs.

They found the old man lying back in the chair where Roger had left him. There was a peaceful expression on his rugged features. On the table by his side lay an envelope addressed to the superintendent and near it stood an empty bottle that had contained pills. The brandy flask was also there, empty.

The unhappy people downstairs were told they could depart as soon as they wished, either then or in the morning. All allegations against them were withdrawn. An explanation was being prepared and would in due course appear in the Press.

"You were with him a long time, Major Bennion," Yeo said. "What did he tell you?"

"Of various episodes in his life," was the reply.

Yeo looked hard at him. Perhaps he guessed something of the truth.

"This will not do much credit to either of us," he said, putting the letter in his pocket.

"I am afraid it will not," Roger agreed, "but perhaps it is the best possible ending."

Roger wrote to his wife Ruth to tell her all that had happened. He said in conclusion—"It has been a truly tragic weekend. Inspector Yeo say it will not do either of us much credit. He may be right. We

167

are told that God moves in a mysterious way His wonders to perform. I cannot help asking myself what would have happened had I not chanced to visit Old Nick's Folly just when I did. So many people were concerned. But we must be content if we are permitted to play our little part in life's great drama."

THE END

Lightning Source UK Ltd.
Milton Keynes UK
UKHW041203040123
414814UK00002B/65

9 781644 399699